Vindicta

Rori Bleu

Rosie Chapel

First printing: 2022
ISBN: 978-0-6454794-9-2 (eBook)
ISBN: 978-0-6457084-0-0 (Paperback)

Ulfire Pty. Ltd.
P.O. Box 1481
South Perth
WA 6951
Australia

Cover Design: R Norman
Cover Image: Canva
Designed in Canva
Internal images: Deposit Photos
Created using appropriate licences

Acknowledgments

Rori Bleu

Special thanks to...

Jean Forrester for helping bring the characters to life, as well as the story.

Terry Fielding for allowing me to spam her mailbox with rough drafts.

Annette Begeschke, **Jo Anne Vesledahl,** and **Sheri Meece** for being forced to continue beta reading.

And to my co-author **Rosie Chapel**... I enjoy writing with you because, I give you a dungeon and a moat for a story, and you transform it into a castle complete with dragons and royal intrigue.

Acknowledgments
Rosie Chapel

Thank you to

Rori for your ongoing insistence that I share your limelight. I keep telling you, you are crazy, but you refuse to listen.

Melanie Duvall — for being kind enough to read the final draft. Your time and quick eye is much appreciated.

As always, special thanks to my hubby for his unfailing support, and for weaving his technical magic to publish the book.

VINDICTA

Rori Bleu

Rosie Chapel

Chapter One

Winter was unusually harsh this year, but the blizzard, now in its second day, blew through Donner Pass with a fury the old timers were comparing with the Friday the 13th Storm of November 1931.

Curled up in her blanket, Bobbi Jo Fletcher was sitting on the couch with the family's mutt, Butch. The old dog had his head on her knee, *protecting* the girl from the raging tempest on the other side of the door.

The duo were doing their best to stay warm in the little house they shared with the rest of the family. The structure once served as a boarding house for the Chinese immigrants the Southern Pacific had hired to complete this stretch of track.

While, for the most part, it was comfortable, thanks to the kerosene heater strategically placed in the center of the living room, the cold winds managed to seep around the door and the window frames.

In the guise of listening to *Dragnet* on the radio, Bobbi Jo was busy eavesdropping on her parents' argument.

"Dammit, John Fletcher, why did you drag us to this Godforsaken shack? You were so close to tenure in Los Angeles."

John Fletcher was no foreigner to a dramatic turn of phrase, if fitting.

"Lois, please, not this again. Were my first three-hundred reasons unclear? How could you expect me to take another day of being stared at by students whose eyes were as dead as the Latin I was trying to instill in them? The only thing they wanted to hear was the bell."

"But why here, John? We could be stuck on this mountain for weeks, if not months!"

"With plenty of supplies, my love. Besides, this is the perfect chance for me to write my novel. I promise it will be a best seller and we can move anywhere *you* want."

Doubtful of her husband's reassurance, Lois marched over to the kitchen sink and stared through the window. The snow was becoming heavier.

Cars still risked the pass in hope of reaching the sunny Pacific coast, but their numbers were dwindling. Lois knew it would not be long before the state police closed the road altogether, leaving them isolated from civilization.

She spun around, the hem of her red gingham dress rippling about her calves, and faced down the man to whom she had been married for the last ten years.

With a huff, she threatened, "If I have to spend even *one* more winter in this house, I swear I will pack the children up and—"

Bobbi Jo's older brother, by all of ten months, raced into

the kitchen, crying. "Please, Mommy, dun leave Daddy. I dun want you to diborce."

A new combatant entering the fray was more than Lois Fletcher could take.

Exasperated, she pinched the bridge of her nose to fight off the pending headache. "What are you talking about, Jimmy?"

"You and Daddy are gonna get a diborce."

"It's divorce, and where did you hear that word anyway?"

"I heard it on one of the radio programs you listened to, Mommy," the boy wailed through his tears. "Please dun get a divorce."

Lois muttered, "Oh for crying out loud."

With a sigh she tried to explain to the child who was far too young to understand. "Do not worry. Your father and I are not going to get a divorce...nor are we splitting up. Sometimes adults disagree on things."

It was no help. The child was inconsolable. "Just like on the radio?"

"James Douglas Fletcher," Lois' tone pierced her son's conviction that the end of his family was nigh. "You are grounded from the radio for a week."

"B-but," the boy stammered.

"Do you want to make it two?"

"Mommy, you're a meanie." Jimmy yelled, and fled the kitchen.

Lois chased after him. "Jimmy, wait."

The boy refused to listen and made a beeline for his bedroom. He slammed the door behind him, triggering a standoff between mother and son, which led to dinner being late.

While the struggle continued down the hallway, the

elder Fletcher joined his daughter in the living room. Shooing the drowsy dog off the couch, he plopped down next to Bobbi Jo.

Butch grunted at the audacity of the human to move him from the comfy warmth of his favorite person. Surmising the bedrooms were chillier than the living room, he elected to pad about the heater before stretching out in front of it.

The pair chuckled at Butch's antics, then John asked, "So, what are we listening to, Squirt?"

"I would say *Father Knows Best*, but after hearing you and mommy, I gotta doubt my father does." Bobbi Jo giggled. Even at her tender age, she was already developing her father's biting sarcasm.

They heard Sergeant Joe Friday break in with his iconic, "Just the facts, ma'am."

"Cops and robbers, huh? Probably a better choice...less dangerous," John quipped.

"Momma gonna make you sleep in the doghouse tonight?" Bobbi Jo snuggled against her father who chuckled.

"Brrrr...I hope not, Squirt, I'd turn into one of your snowmen. Even Butch saw sense hours ago and, instead of constantly digging himself out, came in where it's warm. Pretty sure he's packed his bags ready to move to San Diego."

"Daddy, you're so funny, but we found him in Arizona, so I'm guessing the Grand Canyon."

John Fletcher had taught his children the states of the country and important places there. It was preferable to teaching college students.

A confrontation on the radio silenced their banter.

*The Los Angeles police had a man cornered in a
warehouse who was threatening to shoot any copper
who dared to take a step closer.*

*Sergeant Friday yelled, "Don't be a fool. There's no
way you can escape. Surrender, and I'll see you get a
fair trial."*

*The sound of two shots cracked through the speakers
before the bad guy shouted, "Never, Friday. You'll
never take me alive."*

"If that's the way you want it, Johnson."

Gunfire erupted.

In her mind's eye, Bobbi Jo pictured the police unloading their pistols at Johnson, his body flinching as each bullet struck him. She imagined him sinking to his knees before tumbling, face first, onto the dirty warehouse floor.

While her brother ended up with nightmares if he listened to programs like this, it never bothered Bobbi Jo.

She knew the bad guy was only playing dead. He would be back on the show next week as a patrolman or a witness providing the vital piece of information to help solve whatever crime fell to Sergeant Joe Friday's department.

Her father held an opposing opinion.

"I don't think you should be listening to this show. Too realistic. How about I turn on *Dick Tracy* instead?"

"And have nightmares about the bad guys there? Have you ever seen Flattop Jones in the comics? No, thank you."

Her father shook his head, and tousled her blonde hair, muttering, "You're too smart for your own good, you know that, Squirt."

Both watched Lois, who had given up coaxing her barricaded son from his room, come in and slump into the easy chair usually reserved for her husband.

Not caring who was paying attention, she decreed, "That boy will either come out and eat with us or starve to death."

"Don't you think a death sentence is a little severe, dear?"

His wife did not get a chance to answer.

A loud knocking put paid to that.

The trio in the living room swiveled to face the front door. A brief pause and the sound resumed, although now more an insistent pounding than a cordial rap.

Butch's ears flattened and, instinctively, he crept closer to the couch.

Jimmy flew into the living room, squealing, "Mommy, Daddy there are a bunch of guys out there."

His bedroom faced the front of the house, giving him the best views of any visitors...a rare occurrence at the best of times...inconceivable in weather like this.

"Can I open it?" Jimmy raced to the door.

"James Fletcher," his mother's tone stopped the boy in his tracks. "Sit next to your sister and let your father answer the door."

The boy grumped, "Geez, I never get to do anything exciting in the dumb ol' house."

Grudgingly, Jimmy did as he was told and, after purposely bumping into Bobbi Jo so she would shift along, peeked over the back of the couch, eyes glued on his father.

Unlike her son's excited ogling, Lois cast a concerned

glance at her husband. *This* was one of the reasons she dreaded living in the middle of nowhere.

In the midst of a blizzard you can't turn anybody away. Would be the justification John would use, if she objected to him opening the door.

To do so would mean certain death for whoever it might be.

Her husband was already approaching the door.

John Fletcher was no fool either. He knew the dangers of his family's situation, and kept a shotgun leaning against the doorframe... just in case.

Before inviting in any of those on the other side, he asked, "How may I help you?"

A deep voice on the other side responded, "Mister, please, let us in? We had a car accident a couple of miles back, and have been trying to find somewhere to shelter until this damn weather clears. Please, we're freezing."

"If I give you my shovels, do you think it is possible for you to dig yourselves out?" John countered.

"Mister, please, the snow is blinding. I'm sure if we tried searching for it now, it'd be spring before we found it."

Looking back at his wife, John saw her nod reluctantly. He picked up the loaded shotgun, and pointed the barrel toward the floor, his thumb resting against the hammers.

Unlocking the door, he yelled, "Come on in...slowly."

As soon as the door creaked open, the howling wind whooshed it wide, and it smacked the wall with a solid thud. Four men, caked in snow, stumbled in.

The last to enter, grabbed the knob and put his shoulder to the wood, trying to muscle it shut.

Old Man Winter had no intention of letting a puny human leave him outside. Inhaling deeply, he unleashed an eighty-mile an hour gust of wind, tearing the door from the young man's grasp. His gold ring got snagged on the locking mechanism, reducing his finger to a nub. His gut-wrenching cry was drowned out by the savage storm.

The gale hurled the digit across the floor and it skidded to a bloody halt in front of Lois's chair who, despite serving as a nurse in the war, was unable to stifle a shocked scream.

The three others, along with Fletcher, were scattered about the room like paper dolls, as the snow piled up with frigid rapidity, hampering every attempt to close the door.

It took the burly shoulders of the newcomers several tense minutes to coerce the door shut. Turning in tandem, the three found themselves staring down the double barrels of Fletcher's shotgun, accompanied by a snarling hound.

The oldest of the men, threw up his hands. "Woah, woah, woah, bud. We mean you no harm, I promise. We just need a place to wait out the blizzard."

John studied the three in front of him, their attire...dress coats and hats...entirely unsuitable for the current weather.

"Butch, couch," Fletcher ordered, and the dog slunk away, growling low in his throat.

The shotgun leveled at the visitors, John asked, "Where are you all headed?"

Once more the older man, his hands raised for John to see, spoke, "We were on our way to Sacramento from Reno for an insurance convention. We knew it was snowing up here, but didn't expect to run into this."

"Yeah, it can get pretty brutal up here quickly," John agreed.

In the corner of his eye, he saw the fourth man cradling his mangled hand, blood spurting from the missing finger. He could hear Lois coaxing him, "Sir, please open your hand so I can see the extent of your injuries. I can't help you otherwise."

John took her actions as tacit permission to lower his weapon.

The older man had little sympathy for his companion. "Roy, suck it up already," he admonished brusquely.

Lois interjected, "Sir, your friend has lost his finger and if I can't stop the bleeding, there's a good chance he'll go into shock. So, please be quiet and let me do what I can for him, but we'll have to get him to a doctor as soon as possible."

Giving Lois the stink-eye for daring to interfere, the man mustered up an apology all the same. "Beg pardon, ma'am. I didn't know how bad he was hurt, and I'm sorry he's putting you out."

"He's not the annoying one now is he?" Lois reprimanded.

John deemed it prudent to head off the mounting confrontation between the two. "Name's John Fletcher and you've met my wife, Lois."

"Sorry for my bad manners. The name's Buchanan... Edward Buchanan." Nodding his head to the two standing behind him. "This is Daryl and that's his brother Clarence."

Both men bobbed their heads in silent acknowledgement of their introductions.

"It's nice to meet you...circumstances and all," John replied.

Jimmy could not contain himself any longer. Bounding from the couch with his hand extended, he greeted the men like the local *Welcome Wagon*. "My name is James Douglas Fletcher, and I am almost seven years old."

Buchanan smiled down at the boy, and shook his hand. "It's an honor to meet you, Master Fletcher."

Jimmy beamed at being addressed this way. "And that lump of blanket on the couch is my sister, Roberta

Josephine. It's too hard to say her whole name, so we just call her Bobbi Jo."

Buchanan glanced at the girl on the couch with a toothy smile, but only received a cool stare in return.

Bobbi Jo believed her mother to be good judge of character and whatever *she* felt about the men, Bobbi Jo would imitate.

The sudden chill in the room was even more overwhelming than the wind which had blown the refugees into the Fletchers' house. In an effort to break the mood, John piped up, "I'm sorry for being a poor host. Please, take off your overcoats and hats, and I'll hang them by the heater to dry out."

Buchanan waved his hand behind his back, a signal to the other two to decline the offer.

"If it's all the same to you, Mr. Fletcher, we don't really want to inconvenience your family any more than necessary. If you don't mind, we'll keep our coats, but I will accept your offer to defrost my hat." He removed it, exposing a graying, military-type haircut.

Daryl and Clarence sported similar cuts in differing shades of brown.

John took the hats, thinking their desire *not* to shed their wet overcoats was odd, but gave up wasting his energy working out why. Doubtless the material was more waterproof than he thought, and perhaps the men believed the body heat created by their trek from the car was preferable to the cold which now enveloped the living room.

Jimmy chimed in. "Daddy, shouldn't you give them coffee?" It was something he had heard on the radio. Without fail, the characters in the various shows sounded happy when it was offered, and Jimmy was certain this situation called for it.

"You're right, Jimmy," Fletcher allowed. "I imagine you must be hungry, as well. It isn't much, but please feel free to join us."

"If you don't think it's too much of an inconvenience," Buchanan replied.

"None whatsoever. And while you all eat, Lois will make up places for you to spend the night."

Being demoted to scullery maid, elicited a scornful glare from his wife. John, as he was wont to do, ignored it.

A booming voice from the radio filled the room, "This just in to the KTY news desk—"

"Bobbi Jo, switch off the radio and help me set the table." Fletcher spoke over the report, sending his daughter to the wooden chassis. As she flicked the dial before the man behind the microphone issued whatever report was important enough to interrupt the intro to *Gunsmoke,* she noticed the one called Buchanan had blanched.

Her father brushed off the bulletin. "No doubt a worthless weather report to prevent anybody else from venturing out into the snow."

"Yeah," Buchanan conceded dubiously. "No, doubt."

Chapter Two

January 13, 1952

The blizzard did not relent. By morning, the drifts had reached the bottom of the windowsills and Butch's doghouse was obscured completely.

John was surprised to see Buchanan sitting in one of the kitchen chairs, watching Lois examining Roy's hand.

"Have you both been up all night with Roy?" he asked curiously.

Without skipping a beat as she worked, Lois replied, "I heard a rumble from the mountain earlier. I'm guessing there was an avalanche farther down the ridge."

"Must have been from my snoring, huh?" John's attempt at humor fell on deaf ears.

Judging from the pallor on the young man's face, John surmised Roy must be in agony. "How are you doing?" he asked, his cheerful question at odds with the scene.

Roy's answer was a moan of pain.

Lois shook her head in resignation, informing her husband in undertones, "I stemmed the bleeding long

12

enough to stitch the wound closed. My concern is that gangrene may set in before the storm subsides and, if it does, I don't have any penicillin to treat him."

Buchanan observed heartlessly, "Told him time and again to get rid of that damn ring, but he always said no. Apparently it's some cheap gift from a girl who dumped him. Reckon he got what he deserved."

"Excuse me, Mr. Buchanan," Lois fumed. She had spent the better part of the early hours grappling with the wound and now it appeared her efforts were unappreciated. "Is that any way to talk about one of your employees?"

"Employees?" Buchanan countered, without thinking.

"Yes, Roy does work for you, doesn't he?" Lois rejoined.

"Oh, yeah. 'Cept he works in another office outside of the city. Real estate is lucrative right now around Carson City."

"Carson City? I thought I heard you say you were traveling from Reno to Sacramento for an insurance conference." John canted his head as he questioned Buchanan.

"I'm afraid you misunderstood last night," Buchanan backpedaled. "In all the excitement I can understand. We're heading to Sacramento for a symposium on real estate insurance for real estate agents. My boy Roy there works out of our Carson City office."

Neither deaf nor stupid, John was not in the slightest convinced by the older man's revised story. He knew what he had heard the previous day, but thought it prudent to bite his tongue and let Buchanan think he had accepted his word as gospel.

"How about while Lois deals with young Roy, I fry you and the brothers a good breakfast. I am not quite the cook my wife is, but can manage to crack eggs without breaking the yolks."

"Sounds tempting, Fletcher. I think the boys are still asleep, and I'd hate to wake them. Not morning people, you know."

"No, problem and, please, call me John," John summoned up a friendly smile.

"Sure, John," Buchanan acknowledged without reciprocating.

Hearing her husband's offer to make breakfast, Lois checked the clock above the stove and noticed it was past nine.

"John, since you are cooking for Mr. Buchanan, make sure to fry a couple of eggs for the kids as well. I'll go get them up."

Wiping her hands on her apron, Lois realized it was smeared deep red from Roy's blood...not something children needed to see. She untied it, and draped it over the back of one of the chairs.

With a bright smile, she left the kitchen and padded quietly through the living room, noting the brothers beginning to stir.

Frying bacon...never fails. Lois's mouth twitched in amusement.

Walking down the hall, she stopped at Jimmy's bedroom first. Knocking lightly, she peered around the door to see her son sprawled across his bed, snoring as loudly as his father.

Lois went over to wake him, shaking his shoulder gently. "Jimmy, daddy is making breakfast. You better hurry up and get dressed unless you want to end up with cereal."

The boy mumbled unintelligibly, "Breakfast...bed?"

She pulled the covers off of him, explaining, "Only if you can figure out how to get your bed out to the table. Otherwise, get dressed."

Leaving her grumbling son to decide whether he could actually move the bed, Lois continued on to Bobbi Jo's room.

When she opened the door, Butch's head shot up from his protective position on the bed. Recognizing Lois, he wagged his tail in welcome.

"And a good morning to you too, Butch." Lois returned the salutation by scratching the dog's ear. "Should we wake her up?"

Butch did not need to be told twice, giving Bobbi Jo a sloppy lick across her face.

"Ewww...Butch that's disgusting," Bobbi Jo objected, rubbing the slobber from her face before she peeled back her eyelids.

Lois smothered a laugh. "Hurry up and get ready for breakfast before your brother eats all the bacon."

"He better not," Bobbi Jo warned. "Not if he knows what's good for him."

"Then let's get you dressed."

Mother and daughter spent a few moments chatting whilst deciding on an outfit.

Lois insisted Bobbi Jo would look pretty in her floral-print dress, but the little girl refused vehemently, arguing her overalls would be warmer, folding her arms to emphasize her resolve.

Not in the mood for a repeat of the performance Jimmy had subjected her to the night before, Lois relented in hope of motivating her daughter to get dressed.

Some battles were not worth fighting.

John finished browning the bacon, and began preparing the grease in the pan to cook the eggs. Cracking two into the skillet, he let them sizzle as they began to fry.

The house was filled with a savory aroma, tempting Jimmy out of his room and to the kitchen table. Picking his knife and fork up, he said to his father, "I am ready when you are, and may I listen to *Comic Weekly Man* because I gotta wait so long?"

John leaned over to flip on the counter-top radio. "Sure. Just promise you won't wither away beforehand."

The announcer on the radio was concluding the morning sport scores, "...and in the NBA All-Star Game, the Western Conference defeated the East 79 to 75."

Hearing the radio, Buchanan snapped, "What do you think you're doing? Did I say you could turn on the radio?"

He reached for the knob as John objected, "I don't believe I need to ask you for permission to—"

"To repeat our top story," the announcer interrupted in a stern voice. "In a daring escape from the Reno County Jail, four men overpowered sheriff's deputies who were readying them for transfer to the Nevada State Prison in Carson City. Two of the deputies were murdered during the break, while a third was taken hostage at gunpoint in his green 1950 Packard."

John and Buchanan's eyes locked as the announcer went on, "According to law enforcement officials, the notorious bank robber, Eddy Buckman, AKA Edward Buchanan, led the others to freedom.

"The men were last seen driving toward the California border. Residents and motorists are warned these men are armed and dangerous. If you encounter them, do not try to apprehend, call local police immediately."

John saw Buchanan reach inside his suit coat. Acting on

instinct and a sense of self-preservation for his son and himself, John grabbed the pan from the stove and flung the hot fat at Buchanan's face.

The man yelled in pain as the burning grease scorched the left side of his face. His skin blistered quickly, while the sight in his eye was reduced to a bloody red hue.

Stumbling backward to avoid the frying pan Fletcher was swinging at his head, Buchanan jerked his pistol from his inner pocket, hitting his hand on the counter as he did so. A wild shot erupted from the snub-nose revolver.

Through the searing pain, Buchanan bellowed, "Clarence, don't let the bastard get his gun."

As John ran headlong into the living room to grab his shotgun, he failed to see the stray bullet pierce Jimmy's head, behind his left ear,

What he did notice was his daughter's frozen terror in the hallway and barrels of his shotgun being turned towards her.

Throwing himself in front of Bobbi Jo, John heard the roar of the old gun and felt the bite of the birdshot tear through his flesh. His dying eyes caught specks of blood marring Bobbi Jo's face, but he would never know whose it was.

Bobbi Jo screamed as the pellets which missed her father embedded themselves in her cheek. With trembling fingers, she touched her face, confused by blood dripping off her palm.

A loud click clawed through the haze in her brain, and she peered across the room. The figure, pointing something at her, appeared miles away.

Her brain shrieked at her to run, but she could not move.

Suddenly, she was yanked backwards, at the same time as she saw a fiery flash from the figure's hand.

Bobbi Jo's head lolled, and she saw her mother screaming, but the words sounded distorted. Glancing at where she had been standing, Bobbi Jo saw a puff of plaster billow from the wall, leaving a neat hole in its place.

The girl thought it was a magic trick and wanted to show her mother.

Before she had a chance, Butch charged around her toward the figure holding the mystical firebreather. In slow motion, she watched Butch lunge at the outstretched arm, sinking his teeth into it.

"No, Butch," she mumbled. "Don't be a bad dog."

As her mother pulled her around the corner into the hallway, Bobbi Jo heard another boom, followed by a whimper. She recognized it as the one Butch used when being scolded.

"I told him to behave, Mommy. Please don't be mad at him."

Lois did not reply to her daughter's plea to be merciful to the family's pet. Instead, she banged Bobbi Jo's door shut, and did something she had always forbidden her daughter to do. She fastened the i-hook and, aware there was no key in the outer portion of the lock, clicked the thumb switch up, securing the door.

With all the strength she could muster, Lois pushed Bobbi Jo's dresser against the door. She was not sure how long it would keep the men at bay, but any obstacle which prevented them bursting into the room was a gift from God.

Turning to her daughter, Lois registered that in her panic, she was scaring Bobbi Jo and, despite not having the luxury of time, made a valiant effort to calm down enough to explain what she was about to do.

Hastening to the girl's closet, Lois rummaged through the cluttered depths which represented Bobbi Jo's interpretation of cleaning her room. She found her daughter's green snowsuit balled up in the corner.

Tossing it on the bed, she said, "Hurry up and put your snowsuit on so we can go play outside."

She turned back to the closet to find the girl's boots, hearing the child whine, "It's too cold to go outside, Mommy. Mommy, what's going on? I don't understand."

"Hush now, and do as I ask," Lois replied in tones that brooked no argument.

"Goddammit, Clarence, how could you miss that girl?" Buchanan staggered into the living room, Lois's apron pressed against his eye in a fairly futile attempt to remove the grease. No matter how often he wiped it and blinked, he could not get that eye to focus.

Clarence defended his failure, "Boss, you must have seen that damned dog attack me."

"Look at my face, you ass, I can barely see anything. Get your miserable hide down that hall and take care of the other two. Take that idiot brother of yours so you don't botch it up again."

Resentfully, Clarence did as he was told. Waving his pistol toward the hallway, he signaled Daryl to follow him. The two made their not particularly stealthy way to the other end of the house.

Out of Buchanan's earshot, Clarence groused to his brother, "He pushes me anymore and I'll put a bullet in that ugly mug of his."

Daryl barged passed his brother to check the first door. "Who'da thought it could get worse lookin'?" he joked.

He peered around the jamb to see a medium sized bedroom, complete with a wrought iron bed from another era and a couple of battered wooden dressers. He figured this was the parents' bedroom.

Pausing to listen for any strange sounds, Daryl could only hear the wind battering against the lead glass window. Satisfied the room was empty, he backed out, bumping into Clarence who he punched in the shoulder for standing in the way.

About to open the next door, the duo heard a commotion coming from the room farther down the hall.

"Mommy, I'm scared!"

"Do what I tell you, Roberta, and everything will be okay," Lois soothed.

The fact her mother had used her given name told Bobbi Jo things were anything but okay. She tried to ask questions, but it was hard enough to breathe through the second scarf her mother had wrapped around her head, let alone try to form a coherent sentence.

The pair froze when they heard a fist pounding on the door.

"Open this goddamn door," one of the men bawled.

Lois saw the door knob jiggle, aware it was only a matter of time before the door was forced open. Stuffing Bobbi Jo's head into her red, knitted stocking cap, she tugged the child's mittens on, and ushered her to the window.

By sheer effort of will, Lois opened the snow-caked

sash. The biting cold stung her skin and, to make matters worse, Bobbi Jo fought against being pushed out of the window into the waiting snow bank.

Turning her daughter to face her, Lois cajoled, "Listen to me, Bobbi Jo, you need to be very brave and do as I say—"

The sound of a gunshot splintering the door's lock meant she had mere seconds to get her daughter to understand.

"Those bad men out there are coming to hurt us. I want you to run...run as fast as your little legs will carry you."

Tears spilled out of Bobbi Jo's eyes, smearing the blood on her cheek and soaking her scarves.

"Run to the tracks. There are always trains coming by, Bobbi Jo..." Lois could not hold back her own tears, the icy wind freezing them to her face as they fell.

Several thuds came from the other side of the door and Lois realized they were using their shoulders like a battering ram. Giving Bobbi Jo one last kiss on her nose, she pushed her daughter out of harm's way.

Bobbi Jo hurtled through the hip-deep snow, only to stop when her mother's scream rivaled Old Man Winter's howl. She turned to see Lois disappear from the window at the same time as she heard a gunshot.

The same window was lit by a bright flash, and a plume of snow billowed up as a bullet sank into it, sending the girl fleeing in the direction of the pass.

Clarence lost sight of the child in the blustery snow. Slamming the window closed, he locked the sash.

Glancing at Lois who lay prone on the floor, blood

seeping out from under her body, Clarence shrugged and remarked heartlessly, "It's cold enough in this room to keep her from smelling the place up. We should get the other two and leave them all here."

"Better than looking at them until the snow stops, I guess."

The brothers returned to the living room to collect the bodies of John and Jimmy.

Buchanan grabbed Clarence by the back of his coat. "What do you clowns think you're doing?"

"We're making sure the happy family has some alone time together. What the hell does it look like we're doing?"

"So you took care of the mother and that little brat?"

"Mom took care of the daughter for us."

"What? She murdered her own daughter?" Buchanan was flabbergasted by the thought the woman had it in her to kill the girl.

"Well, she might as well have. Shoved her out of the window for God's sake."

"Wait? You let the kid get away?"

"Relax, Boss," Daryl reassured. "She's as good as dead. She'll freeze to death before she reaches anybody. Let's move these two, then we'll fix up your face."

Chapter Three

Blindly, Bobbi Jo trudged through the blizzard, eventually brought to her knees by the waist deep snow. Exhausted, she huddled in a ball, panting and crying, accelerating the wind's relentless efforts to freeze her scarf to her face.

She rolled onto her back, hearing the snow crunch beneath her. It sounded different from when it was under-foot. More welcoming and comforting, as though she was lying in bed, safe from the horrors she had witnessed.

Her gaze drifted toward the sky. Fascinated, she followed the path of each flake until it joined its friends already clinging to her, certain she could see their indi-vidual patterns.

Looking past them, she focused on the clouds from which they descended, wondering what time it was. She knew when the sun was midway across the sky, her mom called her for lunch.

But there would be no call today...or ever again.

Mommy...Daddy...even stinky Jimmy...were gone. So

was the sun. In its place, angry dark clouds which not only brought snow to her house...but also death.

Bobbi Jo knew her family would not be making a surprise reappearance. There would be no more roles for them to play in the future...only bitter memories.

The little girl decided there and then, if they could not come to her, she would go to them. Closing her eyes, she nestled deeper into the snow...waiting for the end.

Bark.

She opened her eyes, unsure of exactly what she heard.

Bark. Bark.

Somehow through the din of the storm, she heard Butch, *but wait, wasn't Butch hurt when he bit that bad man? Maybe Butch escaped.*

Narrowing her eyes against the glaring white, she spotted a black dot on the horizon bounding through the drifts, her excitement increasing when the form was close enough to make out.

It was *Butch.*

Clambering to her feet, she screamed, "Here, Butch. I'm here. Come to me, boy."

The dog's barking grew louder and more exuberant.

A snow devil whirled up between them, momentarily obliterating her view, but she could hear his yap, although now, it seemed to be coming from behind her.

Twirling around on the slippery snow, she saw Butch racing away from her. She began to cry again, pleading, "Please, Butch, please stop."

As though the dog heard her command over the howling wind, he paused. Turning his head to look at her, Butch barked, beckoning her to follow, then bounded off.

Confused by the lack of paw prints, Bobbi Jo presumed

the heavy snow was covering them, relieved the dog remained in sight.

After what felt like hours, Butch led her to the train crossing. To her astonishment, the tracks were fairly clear, and, more so, it looked like a train had just passed.

Hearing Butch's bark from down the line, Bobbi Jo squinted in that direction. Through the swirling snow, she caught sight of Butch in front of her.

Her dog seemed to be on the trail of something, because he refused to stop no matter how loud her commands.

It was easier to chase him here.

Running along the rails, she saw a dark shape looming ahead of Butch. Whatever it was appeared to have stopped. Focusing on the dog, she noticed him pacing behind it, impatiently, pausing every now and then to make sure Bobbi Jo had not wandered off the tracks.

Approaching the object, Bobbi Jo realized it was a train, which must have been blocked by an avalanche. She had seen a small one the previous winter, but it had not been serious enough to prevent trains plowing through it. This one must be significantly larger.

Eagerly, she dashed toward it. Now, she and Butch would be rescued, leaving her with at least a trace of her family.

Before Bobbi Jo reached her dog, another snow devil whipped up, lasting longer than the first. Desperately, she fought through it, refusing to allow the blizzard to stop her.

Ice and snow stung her eyes, blurring her vision. With a sudden burst of energy, Bobbi Jo made it to the end of the train, smacking into it with a *thud*.

Rubbing her forehead, she called, "Butch, I'm here, boy."

Only the wind answered.

She peered under the train hoping to see her dog seeking shelter. All she saw were a few barely discernible indentations in the snow...leading nowhere.

Sobs wracked her but, this time, she did not consider giving up. Skirting the rail car, she located a door. With a tug, the little girl managed to slide it open.

Bobbi Jo scrambled up the retractable step into the car, and out of the blizzard. She heard the big engines at the front reverberating throughout the train as they struggled to break free from the deadly grip of Old Man Winter.

The thrum was almost hypnotic, making her drowsy. The warmth invited her to shed her wet, freezing snowsuit.

Creeping through the carriage, she found an empty seat, with a blanket somebody had discarded. Curling up, she fell asleep...her dreams, anything but comforting.

"Ma'am," said the man standing next to Bobbi Jo's seat. "As I explained in the Club Car, the avalanche is preventing us from moving any further."

Bobbi Jo snuggled deeper into the blanket, hoping neither of the arguing adults would notice her, leaving enough of a gap to peek out to watch the interaction between the pair.

During the summer, she came with her father to watch the gleaming trains speed by, and he told her stories about it being the conductors, not the engineers, who ran them.

She had listened to Westerns on the radio where the conductors threw people off the trains for not having a ticket.

The man, addressing the woman with the stinky

perfume and the scary looking fox wrapped around her neck, did not look particularly friendly to Bobbi Jo. She was sure he would enjoy pitching her headfirst into a snowbank.

The woman spoke, "You do not understand the gravity of my appointment in San Francisco. I spent a great deal of money with your company to ensure my timely arrival. I must insist you—"

"Do what, ma'am? Push the train single handedly through the drift? Or better yet, how about I climb under the train and lift it up on my back, and fly us all out of here like Superman?"

The idea of the man attempting such a feat made Bobbi Jo giggle, clapping a hand over her mouth, to muffle the sound.

The woman huffed at the conductor's impertinence, and threatened, "Sir, I will have your job."

He removed his cap and offered it to her. "If you think you can do better, feel free. I guarantee you won't be happy with the pay."

The woman spun about and marched off, never ceasing to express her disapproval about the conductor's attitude, and of the rail company's ineptitude in hiring such a boorish person.

"As for you," the conductor addressed the hump on the seat.

"Please, sir," Bobbi Jo begged, as she pulled off the blanket. "Please don't throw me off the train. My family and my dog—"

The conductor shook his head at the little girl, not interested in whatever game she wanted to play; wondering, absently, why her face was so grubby. "Look, as much as I would love to entertain you, I have two hundred and sixty-five other people aboard this train who I need to take care of until help arrives.

"So, if you want to be helpful," he went on as he began to thumb through his instructions of what was required in emergencies such as this, "please go back to your compartment. I am sure your mommy and daddy are worried about you."

"But, Mister Conductor, you do not understand, my mommy and daddy are—"

To her horror, the conductor walked away, leaving her alone.

Unencumbered by parental guidance, Bobbi Jo explored each of the train cars.

Any adult she encountered seemed uninterested in discovering why a five-year-old was wandering unsupervised. Undoubtedly whispering condescending observations amongst themselves concerning the poor parenting practices exercised by the present generation.

When the stewards summoned the passengers to the Dining Car for dinner, Bobbi Jo inserted herself in the middle of a group. Eating with her brother had taught her never to be last to the table.

This left the attendants to question why they came up one meal short.

At the end of the day, she made her way to the Observation Car, with a couple of blankets in tow. Stretching out on one of the seats, taking care not to jar her sore cheek, Bobbi Jo watched the snow falling, and tried to come up with a plan.

She knew there was nothing she could do until the train was liberated from its own problems.

And problems were exactly what faced those aboard the *City of San Francisco* during the ceaseless blizzard.

The passengers were becoming hostile not only with the staff, but also each other. Rumors spread through the train that Southern Pacific intended to leave them stranded on the pass, and allow the storm to claim them.

Those circulating the rumors used the fact that the winds were now topping ninety miles per hour, buffeting the snow against the cars, rocking them back and forth, as proof no one would come to their rescue.

Monday night marked the thirty-sixth hour of the passengers being marooned on what felt like a frozen planet, millions of miles from civilization.

If they thought it was not possible to suffer a worse fate, time and weather proved them wrong, leaving the unprepared convinced death was at their door.

The engines' supply of diesel fuel was exhausted, plunging the occupants into a freezing gloom; the eerie glow of the emergency lights keeping the impenetrable darkness at bay.

A free for all ensued for the remaining blankets, and whatever food the stewards had not stored away.

Fearing she might witness another massacre, Bobbi Jo pulled on her snowsuit and crawled beneath the seats in the back corner of the Coach Compartment. The gloom protecting her from discovery.

Tuesday was a repeat of Monday. The stewards opened

the Dining Car in the morning, long enough to provide a bowl of oatmeal and water for breakfast.

Bobbi Jo squeezed in behind a family who had a daughter approximately the same age as she. As they approached the serving area, Bobbi Jo tapped the girl on the shoulder and struck up a conversation about the snow.

The steward on duty assumed the girls were together and thought nothing of giving each a bowl.

As had happened the previous day, when the last of the line reached the counter, the steward was short of bowls with barely enough oatmeal to feed everyone.

After eating, Bobbi Jo stayed warm by wandering from car to car. Continually moving, built up enough sweat and heat in her snowsuit to make up for what the storm was claiming from the train.

At lunch, a sign was posted on the Dining Car stating, due to the lack of supplies, food would not be served until dinner.

Hungry, Bobbi Jo followed an old man into the Club Car, and stole a bag of peanuts from the bar. She dashed back to the Observation Car where she devoured the lot, while watching the snow.

As she munched slowly on the salty snack, she noticed the clouds were not quite as dark as before and it looked like the snow was not falling as fast.

Maybe we'll get rescued soon, she thought happily.

As night descended on the castaways, they dined on cold-cuts and cups of water.

There was no lack of discontent among the passengers,

blaming anyone who could be even remotely connected to their situation. Even President Harry S. Truman caught blame for not controlling the weather.

With the food consumed, the passengers were quickly ushered out of the Dining Car so the stewards could secure what little supplies remained.

Most of the passengers stumbled through the shadows to finish the odd morsel, pilfered before the curfew, in the sanctuary of their compartments.

Bobbi Jo waited for the aisles to clear then snuck back to her hiding place in Coach.

Opening the door to the car, she took a few steps inside before she froze in her tracks. A deep rumble, reminding the girl of an angry bear, echoed in the darkness, and she recognized it as someone snoring near the back, rivaling the noise her father made.

She knew better than to creep any closer to retrieve her blankets. It was a foregone conclusion that whoever invaded her sanctuary had no doubt stolen those as well.

Backing up, Bobbi Jo kicked an empty bottle, probably discarded by the intruder. It spun, and the rattle of glass disturbed her unwanted guest.

He gave a sudden snort. "Who the hell is there?" a slurred voice demanded. "Show yourself dammit. I have a gun."

Bobbi Jo said nothing, choosing to flee to Second Class.

Finding an empty water closet, she locked the door before huddling on the floor where she tried to sleep.

The hoot of a train horn in the distance, roused Bobbi Jo from her restless night.

She could not understand why the engineers would blow their horns. Surely they understood doing so could trigger another avalanche.

Sitting up, she heard the whistle blare again. Closer than before. Bobbi Jo heard people running along the cars, cheering that their rescue was at hand.

Cracking the door ajar, she poked her head out to see a crowd of people gathering further down the line.

Stepping into the Second Class aisle for a better look, she was immediately swept up in a surge of passengers streaming toward the soldiers and medical professionals sent by the rail company to save them.

Instead of the invective this same crowd had been hurling at their would-be saviors the day before, they were sobbing in relief, and thanking their rescuers.

Extracting herself from the rush, Bobbi Jo sat at one of the dining tables as the conductor and a soldier began to sort through the passenger list in order to transfer the injured and elderly first, followed by the remaining travelers.

For the better part of the morning people were shuttled out of the pass via the military's M29 snow vehicles.

When the conductor reached the end of his boarding list, he noticed a lone passenger in the Dining Car. Seeing it was a child, he hastened to her.

He recognized her as he approached. "Little girl, why are you still here? Where are your parents?"

The strain of holding her grief in check for the last three days, had taken its toll. Tears brimming over, Bobbi Jo wailed forlornly, "I tried to tell you before, bad men killed them."

The conductor's heart sank, and it dawned on him that

what he had assumed to be a sooty smudge on her cheek was, in fact, dried blood. Whisking her into his arms, he took her to find a nurse...and the police.

The proper authorities raced up Highway 40 to the small house on the mountain the girl had identified as hers. They came across the green Packard one of the plows had uncovered and left abandoned along the road in the army's haste to save the passengers of the *City of San Francisco*.

A thorough inspection of the car revealed the body of the missing deputy wedged in the trunk, a bullet to his temple.

Reaching the Fletcher residence, they found the place empty...with the exception of the frozen bodies of the Fletcher family.

The official report stated whoever had committed the crime must have escaped through the cleared pass in the Fletchers' Chevy Suburban.

With little to go on, the trail quickly went cold...as did Bobbi Jo's future.

Chapter Four

Bobbi Jo's Childhood

Bobbi Jo's formative years did not improve with time. After spending three months as a ward of the state of California, relatives, officials judged satisfactory to raise the little girl, were located.

Sent to Minnesota to live with her mother's sister, Florence, and her husband, Olaf, the child learned quickly how little they cared for her.

The couple already had five children of their own whose needs had to be met before that of an unexpected extra.

Bobbi Jo's substitute siblings went out of their way to torment her. Any chores deemed unworthy, they dumped on Bobbi Jo. It could be anything from feeding the chickens, to hauling buckets of water between the pump and the garden, or slopping the hogs.

While she detested every moment of the forced farm labor, it helped her body grow lean and strong.

As for her formal education, it came down to a heated

conversation at the kitchen table. Olaf was adamantly opposed to it, determined to keep Bobbi Jo out of school and on the farm.

"Ain't no need ter squander good money educatin' her," Bobbi Jo overheard him say as she eavesdropped. "We're jus' gonna end up marryin' her off to some short-sighted sucker who won't care about that scarring, when she's old enough."

The girl bit her tongue to stifle her vociferous opposition to that idea. She had seen her own parents argue about things she did not quite understand, as well. These two did not appear any better. Bobbi Jo was positive she did not want to get married...ever.

"Might as well get use out of her 'fore hand."

"Ya have a point there, Olaf," his wife concurred. "But we both know the state won't allow that. Would hate ta lose what little she brings in from them...as well as that insurance thingy her old man set up for her."

"Bah," Olaf grouched. "Damn pittance, Florence."

"Still money. 'Sides, we don't need ta buy her any school clothes, the kids have 'nuff hand-me-downs to see her through at least sixth grade. We can figure out what to do with her then."

"I tell ya right now, woman, if she causes any problems, it's on you."

"When ain't it, Olaf Johnson? You ain't set foot in that school since Elmer was in kindergarten and he missed the bus."

With that, it was agreed to enroll her in the kindergarten with their youngest daughter, Cynthia, despite Bobbi Jo being a year older than her cousin...and every other kid in the class.

The school counselor and principal also felt this was

appropriate, because Bobbi Jo had missed too much school between the death of her family and her *proper* placement with a good Christian family.

This decision proved disastrous from the get-go.

Kindergarten was brain-numbingly boring for her. Everything the teachers taught were things she had already learned from her father. She knew her alphabet and how to write her name. She could count well past one hundred, and understood simple math.

Time and again, Bobbi Jo was reprimanded for rushing through her assignments before the teachers had finished explaining the directions.

This led to her disturbing the rest of the class.

During recess, the larger boys targeted her for making their peers look stupid. While they pushed her around, usually into a puddle, Cynthia led the chorus of chants mocking Bobbi Jo for having an ugly scar, dead parents, and that it was shame she hadn't died too.

First and second grade offered no reprieve.

The teachers viewed the child as annoying and argumentative. Her classmates accused her of cheating when she scored perfect marks in tests.

When Florence asked her daughter why she failed to get the same grades as Bobbi Jo, the girl alleged her cousin was pitied by the teachers because she was an orphan.

Things came to a head when, in the third grade, Bobbi Jo started getting into fights with the other kids. For the most part, she got her ass kicked but, in the process, she learned how to defend herself.

After a test, which most of the class failed miserably, a group of girls, led by Cynthia, decided to teach Bobbi Jo a lesson for achieving top marks.

Cornering her at the far end of the playground, they

taunted her, as usual. Cynthia took it a step further, knowing her mother would be angry that her cousin beat her again.

She picked up a rock and threw it at Bobbi Jo. The impact left a divot in her forehead and splattered blood everywhere.

"Hahaha, now your head matches your stupid face," Cynthia jeered.

Unable to bear anymore, Bobbi Jo lost control.

As the girls laughed at her, Bobbi Jo grabbed the blood-smeared stone, wrapped her fingers tightly around it and punched the nearest of Cynthia's friends in the mouth, breaking the girl's front two teeth.

Her attention shifted to her cousin. Before Cynthia could run away, Bobbi Jo snagged a handful of the girl's blonde hair, and yanked her head back, compelling her to stare Bobbi Jo in the eye.

Fear and tears welled in Cynthia's eyes as Bobbi Jo unleashed a blind fury on her. Despite Cynthia's frantic efforts to avoid the onslaught, Bobbi Jo landed several decent blows.

The girls screamed for Bobbi Jo to stop, but she heard nothing except the sound of splintering bone.

One girl ran to get Mrs. Flynn the playground supervisor.

By the time the teacher arrived on the scene, Cynthia's eyes were swollen shut and her nose was broken. Adding insult to injury, when the woman succeeded in pulling the girls apart, Bobbi Jo flung the handful of blonde hair she had torn from Cynthia's scalp in her face as her cousin crumpled to the ground.

While the school secretary called the ambulance to rush the child to the hospital, Henry Soderberg, the school principal, was on his personal line to her parents, fighting, and losing, his own battle as he tried to explain what happened.

As the attendants of the county's ambulance service placed Cynthia on the gurney, the teachers struggled to usher the children out of the way so the men could wheel her into the back of their army-surplus vehicle.

The rotating red light and large windows, exposing their battered friend to their gawking stares, lured the kids to the ambulance, its cheap white paint peeling to expose an olive-drab undercoat, like flies to honey.

Bobbi Jo saw none of this. Dragged into the building, she was taken to the nurse's office to have her head wound tended to.

The nurse took great pleasure in hearing the child sob in pain when she smeared Merthiolate over the gash on her forehead, before covering the wound with a gauze pad.

From there, she was sent to Mr. Soderberg's office to learn the definition of the school's Corporal Punishment policy.

Soderberg meted out ten whacks with the school's legendary wooden paddle. The last of which was significantly harder than any of the others owing to being berated by an angry parent for failing to protect their child.

Unlike her reaction to the nurse's treatment, Bobbi Jo refused to give the man the satisfaction of seeing her cry. Standing up, she glared at him through red-rimmed eyes, and it took all she had to suppress her tears.

"You are to wait on the bench until your father arrives."

"He's not my father. He's my stupid un—"

"Girl, get your ass on that bench now."

Stamping her booted foot on the wooden office floor, she stomped out to the hallway, to be greeted by the girls who had caused this. Looks between the opposing sides were brief and bitter, but no words were exchanged.

One by one, they were called into the principal's office to give their side of the story. Each repeated the same lie, "We did nothing, sir. She's crazy. She just attacked poor Cindy for no reason."

The last girl slipped up, adding inadvertently, "We were just having fun with her."

Soderberg only heard what he wanted to hear. When Olaf arrived, the two men had a meeting in his office.

"Mr. Johnson, I am sure you can appreciate the severity of what occurred—"

"You mean my precious youngest in the hospital... maybe gonna lose her eye? Yeah, I think I can appreciate it. So how does the school intend to compensate me for the damages?"

"Ex-excuse me?" Soderberg stuttered in disbelief. "What do you mean?"

"For the doctor bills of course. County can't expect me to foot the bills for its school's negligence."

"But, Olaf..."

The two men had known each other since grade school, and Henry knew full well Olaf was not one to lash out with idle threats...especially when there was money to be had.

"...it was a fight between two children...your children at that. You cannot believe the school is responsible for hostilities between siblings."

"Don't *but Olaf* me, Henry. We both know one of them Minneapolis lawyers might see it differently."

Soderberg sank into his chair as the farmer glowered over him.

"I'll let you consider that, Henry, while you tell me what the school has in mind for that little bitch out in the hall."

"At present, all I can do is suspend her for a week, pending a meeting with Superintendent Engstrom and the school board on the matter for expelling her. Personally, I recommend getting that girl professional help."

"Bah, spending more money, I ain't got. I've already taken matters into my own hands." Olaf prepared to leave the office.

With the principal in tow, Olaf stood in front of Bobbi Jo. "Get to your feet, girl, we're going home."

"Why, so you can beat me like you do your own kids?" Bobbi Jo accused him.

Soderberg furrowed his brow at Bobbi Jo for her disrespectful attitude toward an adult...even if it was Olaf Johnson.

Not wanting to deal with county, Olaf quelled the urge to backhand his niece where she sat. Instead, he made do with yanking her up by the arm, and frog-marching the squirming girl to his waiting pickup.

Once they made it back to the farm, the two fell into a yelling match. Olaf's fingers dug deeper into Bobbi Jo's upper arm, leaving dark angry bruises.

Throwing the girl onto her bed, the farmer stalked out, returning moments later with a burlap sack.

Bobbi Jo watched him drop it on the floor in front of him. "What are you planning on doing with that? Throwing me inside and drowning me like you would a cat?" she snarled.

"Would be a fittin' end for ya. I knew you were a bad apple since the day ya set foot on my property. I'm packin' what's yours and moving ya on. I already called your Aunt Mabel in Missouri. I'm sending you down there to be a pain in her ass, and to get ya as far away from my sight as possible. I hope for your sake, she was sober enough to understand what I was saying."

Olaf wasted little time stuffing clothes into the bag. Any personal mementos Bobbi Jo tried to claim, he snatched from her and tossed them away. "You ain't got room or need for that shit."

Once her dresser was empty, Olaf marched Bobbi Jo out to the truck. He pushed her through the driver's side, refusing to relax his grip on her arm, effectively preventing any chance she might escape through the passenger side door.

Firing up the GMC, he drove to the railway station in Mankato.

Not relinquishing his grasp, Olaf hauled her to the ticket window.

"One-way to Saint Louis."

"Coach or First-class?" asked the clerk.

"Do I look like a goddamned Rockefeller? Coach!"

Olaf paid for the ticket, then urged Bobbi Jo to the platforms and the waiting trains. He found the track they needed, as well as the conductor who was studying his watch.

"'S'cuse me, you run this train?" Olaf enquired gruffly.

"If you mean, am I the conductor of this passenger liner? Yes, I am," the conductor answered, annoyed at the hick's blunt attitude.

"Whate'er," Olaf dug into his pocket, pulling a fiver from its depth. "This is yours if you make sure she gets to Saint Louis."

The conductor crooked a brow at Olaf and swung a shrewd gaze back and forth between the man and the girl, who was trying to free herself from his clutches. "And what am I supposed to do with her once we get there?"

"She should have family waiting for her. If nobody meets ya on the platform, just make sure she gets inside the station."

"Seems like a lot of work for a measly five spot."

"Greedy bastard," Olaf mumbled. "Fine, here's another five. Now take her off my hands."

He released Bobbi Jo, and she scooted up the steps of the train, turning long enough to flip him the bird. A gesture, she had learned from her time as a ward of the state.

About to walk away, Olaf informed the conductor, "She's your problem now."

From this point, Bobbi Jo drifted between various relatives. She never lasted more than a year or two with any of them before wearing out her welcome.

It came in the form of fighting in whatever school to which she had been transferred.

By sixth grade, she had stopped bothering to make friends. It saved her from saying goodbye.

She had attended three junior highs by the time she was fourteen. Outwardly, she excelled at her studies, her intelligence far exceeded that of her classmates, while her inner rage burned unchecked.

High school was the last straw for Bobbi Jo.

In her freshman year, she was enrolled in a Milwaukee high school, and living with a woman named Hilde Baker, her father's third cousin, twice removed. The woman was only ten years older than Bobbi Jo, compounding an already tenuous situation.

Hilde worked the night shift in a brewery and left Bobbi Jo to her own devices. This meant the fifteen year old was free to roam the streets at will, with whoever she wanted.

To Hilde's surprise, Bobbi Jo landed a job waiting tables at a diner near the same brewery.

Before long, Bobbi Jo caught the attention of the men who worked with Hilde and, subsequently, the ire of her cousin's female co-workers. Malicious whispers about a young whore at the diner who was sleeping with married men for a few bucks, spread quickly.

Hilde doubted there was any truth to the rumors but, four months into the semester, she was called in front of the high school principal to account for the gossip.

"Miss Baker, please understand, here at Roosevelt High, we take any and all accusations of educational and moral impropriety very seriously," Mr. Taylor, the high school principal began. With that righteous premise, he unveiled the allegations against her ward.

"Roberta is accused of cheating on her midterm test by a very reliable source."

In a vain defense of her academic reputation, Bobbi Jo piped up, "I've never cheated on any test ever," and cast the false charge back at her accuser. "That goddamned Karen is trying to get me expelled because she's afraid I'll take her boyfriend."

"Shut your stupid mouth, Bobbi Jo," Hilde snapped, not wanting the girl to cause any more trouble, but her warning came too late.

"You see, Miss Baker, she has no remorse or decorum. She refuses to accept responsibility for her actions." Taylor wagged his finger at Bobbi Jo. "As though cheating was not bad enough, the gossip in the halls about this girl's promiscuity cannot be ignored either. It is totally unacceptable, and detrimental to the decency of our school."

Taylor pressed the button on his intercom, paging his secretary.

A tired, nasally voice answered, "Yes, Principal Taylor?"

"Mrs. Bertram, please send Gerald Clark into my office."

"Yes, sir."

The office door opened to a fresh-faced junior. His stature was one of a multi-sport letterman, as well as the captain of the football team.

He stood in front of the principal. "Gee, Mr. Taylor, why did I get called into the office?"

He glanced at Bobbi Jo. "Did I do something wrong?"

Taylor smiled at the boy and reassured him, "No, Jerry. I summoned you to help clarify a few things concerning Miss Fletcher."

"I don't know what I can tell you, but I'll do my best."

"Did you see Miss Fletcher cheat on her midterm?"

Gerald was quick to answer, "Don't know anything about the test 'cept what my girl...I mean Karen White said she saw."

Bobbi Jo intervened, "See, Mr. Taylor, hearsay."

Without hesitation, Gerald launched in a neatly fabricated story, "While I may not be able to...what's that word...cooperate—"

"You mean corroborate?" Taylor aided the boy.

"Yeah, that. I can tell you how creepy Bobbi Jo is. She's been following me around and offering to do stuff a good girl like Karen would never think of. Stuff like...geez, Mr. Taylor, I blush even thinking about it. Do I really have to tell you what she said?"

"Please, Jerry, it is important."

"Okay, if you say so. She said she would let me have sex and stuff with her if I'd go out with her."

"That's a boldfaced lie, Gerald Clark, and you know it," Bobbi Jo shot back.

Ignoring Bobbi Jo's outburst, Gerald continued virtuously, "It was pretty awful, sir, especially since I have a swell girl I plan on marrying after college. I heard from some of the other guys on the team that she offered to do the same thing for them. I was shocked, I tell you."

Bobbi Jo's mouth gaped open at the accusation. Rage boiled in the pit of her gut. She scoured her brain for a cutting comeback but before she could form the words, Gerald twisted the knife a little deeper.

"She might think she's cute, but it's all in her head. Those scars don't suggest she's all sweet and innocent, do they? She's got serious mental proble—"

"Okay, Jerry," Taylor, not completely gullible, broke in. "That's enough. You may return to class."

"Thank you, Mr. Taylor. I hope I was of help."

As he moved toward the door, Gerald shot Bobbi Jo a sneer only she saw.

"As you can see, Miss Baker, I have no choice but to severely reprimand Roberta."

Heilde wanted to believe her niece, but the seemingly incontrovertible evidence made it difficult for her to accept Bobbi Jo's side of the story.

"I understand, Mr. Taylor. Do as you see fit."

Obliged to accept a zero on her midterm, it plummeted Bobbi Jo's grade point average from a solid A to a C-. As if that were not humiliation enough, the faculty labeled her a cheat and trollop in private, while the student body publicly branded her Loosey Goosey.

Unable to stand anymore, Bobbi Jo took matters into her own hands.

Given a month's worth of detention, to reflect on her poor life choices and return to the straight and narrow, Bobbi Jo was still at school long after the other students had gone home...all except the jocks.

Every afternoon, after serving her punishment, she hung around the gym until she caught the attention of Gerald Clark...without his clingy girlfriend.

As he left the locker room, she ambushed him.

"Jerry." Her smile, deliberately coy. "Ya know...you were right in Taylor's office. I really do want to show you a good time." Her fingers tiptoed over his chest.

He wanted to say no. He knew Karen would kill him if

she ever found out, but then again Karen never gave out. *Hell, she barely kisses me*, he reasoned inwardly.

Vacillating, he hedged, "You know Karen—"

"What about her?" Bobbi Jo cooed. "What she doesn't know won't hurt her, doesn't mean you have to break up with her or anything."

For a teenage boy in his hormonal prime, the offer of sex with no strings attached was too tempting to pass up.

"Wh-where do you want to go? The backseat of my car?"

"Eww." Bobbi Jo shook her head. "No, I have a better and more private spot in mind."

She took Gerald by the hand and led him into the school's athletic equipment room.

"Get undressed first, stud, and I'll lay out the gym mat for us."

His pants were off before she had finished giving him instructions. While Gerald tugged his T-shirt over his head, Bobbi Jo grabbed a ten pound dumbbell and swung it at his face.

She struck his nose. Blood spurted onto the white cotton staining it red. Howling in pain, he stumbled, falling backward onto the same mat where, moments before, he expected to lose his virginity.

Without dropping the weight, Bobbi Jo straddled his waist and crooned in his ear, her tones mocking, "Well now, that might leave a bit of a dent. If there's a God, Gerald Clark, you'll be left with scars which mark *you* for the creep you are, Mister *Sweet and Innocent*."

Giving him no chance to dislodge her, she sat up straight and twisted around to smash the weight against his knee. By the third sickening thud, a crack echoed around the room, ending any thoughts Gerald might have had about attending college on a football scholarship.

Bobbi Jo was not sure the jerk would even be able to walk again.

After that, she dropped out of school. There had been calls from the boy's family that she be committed to an asylum or, at the very least, be lobotomized to make her more docile and less dangerous.

When Bobbi Jo threatened to tell the police...or at least the local newspapers...he had tried to rape her, the demands subsided.

Free to work full time at the diner, she arranged her shifts to ensure, as far as possible, they were opposite to Hilde's. The two simply passed each other in the doorway.

Notes from Hilde concerning money for rent or food were left on the kitchen counter, along with an envelope in which Bobbi Jo could deposit her share.

It was a system both could live with.

Chapter Five

May 12, 1964

Theirs was a fragile truce, one Bobbi Jo knew was tenuous at best. It lasted...not always amicably... until Bobbi Jo's seventeenth birthday.

She had saved up enough money from her job to purchase a 1953 DeSoto FireDome convertible she had seen advertised in the newspaper.

Bobbi Jo did not bother to say goodbye to Hilde. She simply packed her stuff and left.

In her haste to find a means to escape Milwaukee, Bobbi Jo had not checked out the vehicle properly. The undercarriage had been savaged by the Wisconsin road salt. The body itself was basically held together by rust and the car's faded red and beige, two-tone paint job.

She had scarcely crossed the Illinois border when she discovered why the guy was willing to sell the DeSoto so cheaply.

She stopped at the next gas station, to be informed by

the attendant, "Miss, your radiator is low and looks like it could use a good flush. We just happen to have a special—"

Bobbi Jo was already counting her pennies.

"Just fill it up and sell me some coolant. I'll take care of it when I have time." Ignoring the DeSoto's looming mechanical problems seemed the best solution. *Out of sight out of mind.*

Once the man topped off the rusty reservoir, Bobbi Jo fired up her car and continued on to Chicago, where it was necessary to repeat the procedure, as well as refuel.

Unhappy when she realized how much it was going to cost to shake off her previous life, Bobbi Jo wrestled the shifter into gear, aiming for Route 66 and points west.

The DeSoto decided Bobbi Jo needed to break her journey in St Louis.

Pulling into a service station, she cursed the obstinate vehicle and the bastard who had sold it to her.

Not only was the piece of shit gulping gas like it was water, but the water it *ought* to be holding was pissing out of the radiator like a guy with a bladder problem.

A young man in a spotless white uniform strolled out of the door and over to Bobbie Jo's side of the car, careful to avoid the water pooling under it.

"Howdy, Miss," he greeted, reminding her of a milkman rather than someone who pumped gas for a living.

"I think you might have a problem with your car," he said with cheerful sarcasm, nodding at the front of the vehicle. "What do you want filled first, your gas tank or your radiator? Or should I just put a bullet in the engine block and end its misery?"

"Very funny, asshole. You should take your act to Vegas. I'm sure they'd hate you there too."

The man shrugged. "Since you don't appreciate my humor, what can I do ya for?"

"Fill'er up, and check the radiator," Bobbi Jo relented as she climbed out of the car to stretch her legs.

"For what? Survivors?"

Failing to get a rise from the cute girl, he frowned. "Oh, come on, you have to admit that one was at least worth a chuckle."

"If I do..." Bobbi Jo looked at the name patch stitched onto his uniform, "...Ralph, will you stop?"

Waving her off in disappointment, he wandered to the pump, pausing long enough to ask, "Premium?"

Bobbi Jo shot him a glance in disbelief that he had to ask.

He lifted the hose, acknowledging, "Regular it is."

Inserting the nozzle into the tank, Ralph locked the handle to allow him access to the more pressing problem under the hood.

"Ya really should get this thing replaced."

"Have any free ones?"

"No, but I do have the next best thing."

Ralph disappeared into the station, returning with a bottle containing a dark sludge resembling molasses.

Bobbi Jo had no clue what it was.

Ralph emptied the contents into the leaky reservoir, and then filled it with water. Instantly, the water began to flow out of the bottom.

Paying no attention, he finished filling the gas tank and returned the nozzle to the pump. "That will be three fifty."

"What the hell? The pump says three bucks."

"Yeah, three for the gas and fifty cents for fixing your radiator."

"You're crazy," Bobbi Jo charged. "The radiator is still leaking like a sieve."

"Check it now," Ralph replied casually.

"Don't take me for a fool. You did nothing to fix it. In fact, I think you probably did more damage to it. Thanks for nothing."

Shaking his head, he reiterated, "Just check it out."

Muttering about calling the cops on him, she went to the open hood, startled to note, the radiator was still fairly full. Crouching, she saw only a small puddle where, normally, there would be a flood.

"H-How did you do that? What *was* that crap?"

"A secret recipe I came up with to plug leaks. Calling it *Plugger-Up*."

"Will it hurt my engine?"

"Who knows? Yours is the first one I tried it in. Plus, it couldn't do any more damage to it...I'm guessing."

Bobbi Jo could not believe her ears.

"Whatever," she huffed as she began digging in her purse, "and that's a terrible name."

Extracting a handful of change and a couple of crumpled bills, she counted and recounted the small bundle. It did not take her long to realize paying Ralph would take the remainder of her money.

She hemmed and hawed, scouring her brain to come with a way of settling the account without handing over her last cent.

Eventually, Ralph put his hand up. "Forget it. I'll cover this one for ya. You just have to promise me to let me know how it works."

Bobbi Jo smiled at him, and got behind the wheel, reassuring him, "You have my word."

Seeing her Wisconsin plates, he added, "Oh, before you leave, it takes about twenty-four hours for the stuff to seal properly. Do you have any place to stay in town?"

She arched her brow before replying, "Don't worry, I have people in St Louis, so you don't have to put yourself out, I'll make do."

"If I offered, my girl would have my balls. I was gonna suggest checking out the rooms for rent across the street. The old lady there is a soft touch for stranded females. That way you can leave your car here to cure."

"I've had enough problems with strangers in the past. I'll take my chances with family. You have a payphone around here?"

The lad grinned, "Yes, miss, the booth's round the side of the building. While you make your call, I'll make sure to roll your car into the garage."

Nodding to Ralph, Bobbi Jo headed to the booth, clutching her money. Entering the small cubicle, she closed the door behind her.

With a clatter, she dumped her life savings onto the metal shelf. Picking through the small pile, she found a dime, then paused for a moment, deciding whether it was worth spending it on Aunt Mabel, to whom Bobbi Jo had not spoken since the former had shoveled her niece, unceremoniously, onto a bus to Omaha.

"She's no doubt drunk off her ass already," Bobbi Jo told her reflection in the phone's chrome.

Cupping her hand, she brushed the coins back into her palm and dropped them into her pocket. She exited the booth, and hesitated, eyeballing the place across the street where Ralph had suggested she try to get a room.

It was a two-story clapboard house which, other than needing a freshen up, looked sturdy enough to spend the night in.

Having no other viable option, she walked to the curb and, checking for oncoming traffic, crossed to the other side.

Ralph chuckled to himself as he watched the girl's indecision through the station's large window. When he saw her head across the street, he said, "You better thank me for this one, Miss Gladys."

Bobbi Jo hovered at the front door, continuing to second guess herself about knocking. The rumble of her stomach urged her to action.

Her polite, yet firm, rap was answered by a woman in a red silk kimono and curlers in her bleached-blonde hair, who looked barely older than she. Expecting the proprietor to be much older, Bobbi Jo was taken aback.

The woman smiled. "What can I do ya for?"

"Umm...the guy across the street said you might have a room I could rent for the night."

"Oh, doll, you want to talk to Momma," yelling over her shoulder, "Momma, it's for you."

Looking Bobbi Jo up and down, she added, "Real cutie this one is, too."

The throwaway comment actually made Bobbi Jo blush. As far as she was concerned, the one good thing to come out of her life until recently was that, as a result of a balm given to her at the hospital — all those years ago — and applied regularly, the peppering on her cheek had faded as she got older. The damage inflicted by the pellets had been reduced to a faint pattern of tiny scars...only discernible if you looked closely.

It was kinda nice to hear someone describing her as attractive.

Over the blonde's shoulder she saw a tall, lithe lady in black peddle pusher pants and a bright white blouse, the top three buttons undone to expose the rise of her firm breasts. A click of her heels and she came to stand behind the woman.

"Alice, how many times do I have to tell you not to open the door half naked."

"I have my robe on," Alice objected.

Grasping Alice's arm, Momma directed her to the staircase, "Get upstairs and finish dressing. We open in a couple of hours and I don't need you to look a fright again for our gentlemen callers."

Alice was about to offer a retort concerning the night in question, but a firm swat on her butt sent her scurrying up the stairs.

Slicking her hair back, the woman referred to as Momma towered over Bobbi Jo. A trained eye examined the newcomer briefly. "And what can I do for you?"

"Like I was telling her, the guy across the street suggested I see if you might have a room for the night."

Momma narrowed her eyes at the attendant who was waving to her, a stupid grin on his face.

"Forget it, Ralph," the woman hollered around Bobbi Jo. "You still can't come over. Not 'til you pay up for last time. I still have a hole in my wall. And stop sending girls over like you're a damn recruiter. This ain't an army barracks."

Finished with her tirade, Momma turned her attention

to Bobbi Jo. "Look, sweetie, I don't have the room or need for a new girl. Why don't you try the Y?"

"Cuz my car is broke down across the street and won't be fixed until tomorrow. Ralph said you could put me up. I don't have much, but I'll give you whatever I've got if I can just crash for tonight."

"Did Ralph happen to tell you what we do—"

Bobbi Jo's rumbling stomach interrupted the woman's question.

"Oh, for Chrissakes, get in here before you pass out on my porch. Wouldn't be good for business, and the neighbors would no doubt gossip."

Bobbi Jo stared around her. Except for the service station, this house, and a few scattered warehouses, the street appeared abandoned and forgotten.

"Well, are you coming in or not?" Momma growled. "I don't have all night."

The woman turned her back and walked down the hall-way. "The name is Gladys, but as you heard, the girls call me Momma. Annoying as fuck if you ask me."

Bobbi Jo fell in step behind her, hearing the sound of feminine laughter and chatter drifting from the floor above.

As the two entered the kitchen, they were greeted by a stack of dirty dishes in the sink and no food on the stove.

In a voice, Bobbi Jo swore shook the house, Gladys thundered, "Who the hell pissed off Sadie again?"

From the top of the stairs a voice echoed down, "Who do you think, Momma?"

"Shut up, Betty," another voice rang out.

"Mindy, what did you do now?" Gladys demanded.

"It wasn't my fault, Momma. Sadie started it. She called me a pig just because I brought a couple of plates down this morning."

"You are a pig," Gladys agreed with the missing house-keeper, and scrutinized the girl again with a more discerning eye.

She mouthed a question to Bobbi Jo. "How old are you?"

The lie tripped off Bobbi Joe's tongue, "Twenty-two."

Gladys rolled her eyes, knowing better. She had been in the business long enough to recognize an underaged runaway. Better yet, she was not stupid enough to risk putting one to work upstairs.

Sighing, she closed her eyes and replied to the unseen Mindy, "I'd kick your ass out on the street if you didn't have such marketable features. You have no idea what it took to get Sadie back the last time you two went at it. Don't bitch when it comes out of your pay."

Bobbi Jo tapped the woman's arm. "I'll clean the kitchen for you in exchange for a night."

Canting her head, Gladys considered the value of the offer, adding, "Can you cook as well?"

"I haven't starved to death."

"But is your food palatable?"

"Only one way to find out."

"Fine, I'll give you a shot tonight. But fuck up my kitchen and out you go."

Folding back her sleeves, Bobbi Jo ignored the threat and set to repairing the mess. As she washed, other plates and bowls appeared on the counter behind her. Without a word, Bobbi Jo gathered them up, and dumped them in the suds.

After what felt like forever, she admired a shiny sink and clean countertop.

She heard the front door open, and the sound of a male voice greeting the girls. Given nobody had entered the kitchen, Bobbi Jo was not sure when or how they managed to eat, but she had been tasked by Gladys to provide a meal. So, that's what she would do.

Rifling through the refrigerator and the pantry, Bobbi Jo found everything she needed to replicate Aunt Florence's meatloaf.

The woman might not have given two hoots for Bobbie Jo, but she sure knew how to cook and, the kitchen was the one place when their frosty relationship thawed... just a little.

A fixture at the stove for the next few hours, Bobbi Jo fried the main course for whichever girl wandered in on her break, although none bothered to converse with the cook — she wasn't gonna be there long.

The odd silence...beyond the unmistakeable sounds emanating from whichever bedroom was above the kitchen... was kind of comforting and reminded her of the time she spent in Milwaukee before everything went to hell.

As Bobbi Jo served a girl named Eve, the voice above them screamed, "Oh my God, you're such a stud. The best ever."

The two women in the kitchen looked up at the ceiling, then at each other.

Eve laughed. "She missed her calling as an actress."

"I thought she was getting paid for the number of times she repeated that phrase."

Finishing her meal, Eve handed her plate to Bobbi Jo, saying, "Too bad you're not staying longer. Trying to down Sadie's chow requires a skill I haven't managed to accomplish yet."

"Who says she's leaving?" The question caught the pair by surprise. "The girls have been raving about your cooking all night." Leaning against the jamb, her arms crossed, and a cigarette caught casually between the hint of a smile, Gladys addressed this last to the newcomer.

She exhaled, the smoke mingling with her next words, "So how about it, umm...?" Gladys realized in the rush to open, she had forgotten to ask the girl her name.

In this house, Bobbi Jo was sure nobody was who they claimed to be. Put on the spot, she failed to come up with a clever moniker, and resorted to the one name she had come to detest and seldom uttered herself because others used it in reprimand. "Roberta."

"Nice to make your acquaintance, *Roberta*," Gladys greeted her officially, the slight emphasis on the girl's supposed name letting her know she accepted whoever the new hire wanted to be. "If you could make a decent Manhattan you'd be the complete package."

Already familiar with the alcohol cabinet, Bobbie Jo grabbed a tumbler and the necessary mixers. In a matter of minutes, she was pouring the cocktail into a chilled glass for her new employer.

Gladys looked curiously at the girl as she savored the drink.

"Lived with an alcoholic aunt for a couple of years. Came with the territory, I guess," Bobbi Jo offered in explanation.

"Remind me to have you fitted for a bartender's outfit. I'm putting you out front tomorrow night."

Before the end of the evening, in order to guarantee the girl would stay, Gladys had agreed to replace the faulty radiator in the DeSoto, instead of trusting Ralph's haphazard patch job. In addition, she allowed Bobbi Jo to sleep in the Butler's Pantry.

"Don't worry about privacy," Gladys assured. "None of the girls know we have one, let alone stepped foot in there."

For the next couple of months, these women represented the closest thing to an actual family Bobbi Jo had known, since she was five.

Chapter Six

Bobbi Jo slotted into the household, easily. They all had a history they were running from, but no one cared about the details.

What they *did* care about was Bobbi Jo's cooking.

The early morning aroma wafted up the stairs and permeated the floorboards of the upper story. No matter their state of dress...or undress...it brought everyone into the kitchen. Satisfying their ravenous appetites came before modesty.

Even Mindy eventually came to respect the newest resident of the house; though not after a hard fought war between the two.

In the same way as she had with Sadie, Mindy tried to establish her dominance over Bobbi Jo during the latter's first week. It started innocuously enough.

Plates were returned to the kitchen days after food had solidified onto them. Glasses contained thick milk scum on the bottom of each. It amused Mindy, who knew it would take hours to clean them all.

Mindy was sure Roberta would go running to Momma and beg her to intervene. However, she learned quickly that her housemate was a tougher nut to crack.

At first, Bobbi Jo ignored Mindy's childish pranks, but the third time Mindy pulled the stunt, the new housekeeper decided to take action.

In addition to keeping the kitchen in order, Bobbi Jo had assumed responsibility for the laundry.

Finding a pair of Mindy's red, French pinup stockings in the hamper, Bobbi Jo *accidentally* got them wound up in the washing machine's wringer, causing them to snag and shred beyond repair.

Bobbi Jo apologized profusely. Gladys shook her head, telling Mindy to stop whining and buy another pair.

The battle became one of attrition, and nothing was sacred.

The sleeves on Mindy's favorite cashmere sweater came undone at the seams when she put it on.

Her retaliation came in the mysterious deflation of the angel food cake, which had taken Bobbi Jo most of the morning to prepare and bake.

Bobbi Jo had gone to fetch some spices from the pantry for the dinner she was assembling. At the slam of the oven door, and the sound of heels clattering across the floor, she rushed back into the kitchen in time to see her labor of love collapse.

The coup de grâce crossed a line, demanding a response which, ultimately, decided the victor.

It occurred the night Bobbi Jo had spent the better part of the evening either rustling up food in the kitchen or mixing cocktails in the parlor.

Mindy had overheard her rival singing to herself while she worked.

Bobbi Jo never sang in public, she only did so to soothe her frayed nerves. To perform in front of a crowd made her anxious which manifested in stage fright.

Of this, Mindy was unaware, but the knowledge would have made no difference and, in fact, merely added to her glee.

During the latter part of the evening, when the parlor was full of gentlemen sipping Bobbi Jo's drinks, Mindy sprang up, chirping, "Momma, our talented bartender should honor our guests with a song."

Gladys glanced at the bar and, seeing Bobbi Jo blanch, cocked a quizzical brow. "Why am I only just finding out about this, Roberta?"

"B-because, I really can't sing. Strangled cats sound better."

"Don't believe her, Momma, she has a sweet voice." Mindy had only heard a couple of bars. She guessed the housekeeper had no real talent, and was more a shower singer.

The men in the room cheered Bobbi Jo, offering money. When one of them offered twenty-five bucks, Gladys could hardly refuse the monetary opportunity to exploit her bartender.

"I'm sure you're better than you give yourself credit for," Gladys cooed in her smooth style.

Trapped, with no hope of escape, Bobbi Jo came out from behind the bar. Closing her eyes, she inhaled deeply.

She broke into an acapella rendition of *It Had to be You*. The room came to a halt. While she was far from professional, Bobbi Jo was able to hold her own.

Even her bitter rival stood slack jawed. Begrudgingly, Mindy conceded that Roberta could have given Doris Day a run for her money.

The bartender narrowed her gaze at Mindy as she brought the song to a satisfying conclusion.

Gladys led the roaring applause as she circled the room collecting money.

Bobbi Jo took a quick bow and disappeared into the kitchen.

Busy dishing up plates of her piping hot stew, she heard footsteps come to a stop at the doorway.

She turned to see Gladys in her usual pose, cigarette lit. "Are you gonna let her get away with that?"

"Oh, hell no, Momma," Bobbi Jo replied without pausing in her task.

"Well, just make sure she can still fuck." About to retrace her steps, Gladys added, "Oh, and don't think you can avoid giving another performance. I wonder if there is enough in the budget to hire a combo to accompany ya."

A few days later, a blood curdling scream rang out from the room over the kitchen, waking the house.

Bedroom doors were flung open to locate the source. The occupants, seeing Mindy descending the stairs in a rage, followed hot on her heels.

Clutching her laundry bag, she charged into the laundry room. "You bitch. How could you? Do you have any idea how much I paid for this stuff?"

Humming to herself, Bobbi Jo was folding delicates, making sure nothing was wrinkled.

She faced Mindy, an artless smile tugging at the edges of her mouth. "Whatever do you mean, Mindy?"

"You know damn well." Mindy hurled her laundry bag at Bobbi Jo, who avoided it, with a judicious sidestep.

The bag hit the wall behind the housekeeper, spilling the contents. Formerly white bras and underwear were scattered across the floor, their current hue — a sickening pink.

"I'm not sure what you're upset about? Were they folded wrong?" Bobbi Jo asked.

"No. They were washed with this." Mindy snatched a new, bright red towel from under the pile. The revelation caused collective gasp from those in the doorway, followed by a howl of laughter.

Feigning an expression of shock, Bobbi Jo fought the urge to join in. Innocently, she admonished her accuser, "You should know better than to mix colors with whites... especially something red. You know the machine's hot water—"

"Hot water?" Mindy squealed. "Have you never done laundry before? These all needed to be hand-washed in cold..." the secondary consequence of Roberta's actions, hit Mindy like a gut punch.

Tossing aside the towel, she grabbed a negligee, a gift from one of her prominent customers. Not only was it now pink instead of virginal white but also, as she held it against her, Mindy realized it had shrunk beyond recognition.

Like a wildcat pouncing on its prey, Mindy lunged at Bobbi Jo. The two tumbled to the floor, rolling about in Mindy's underclothes.

The women watching the fray, egged them on.

Succumbing to her usual demons, Bobbi Jo found herself sitting on top of the struggling woman.

Set to reduce Mindy to a sniveling mass of blood and welts, Bobbi Jo raised a clenched fist, only to have her assault thwarted by a vice-like grip on her wrist. A voice penetrated the fog of violence and rage, pulling her back from the brink.

At first, Bobbi Jo thought it was her mother, and tears stung her eyes. Through the watery blur, she discerned Gladys, who had been summoned from her office to act as a referee, glaring down at her.

"Roberta, enough," Gladys commanded.

Abruptly, the fight left her, and she crumpled off her opponent.

Gladys barked, "The rest of you, upstairs. I will deal with you all later."

A repeat of the order was not required. They fled up to their bedrooms in a quest for safety.

Blending in with the melee, Mindy attempted to escape, to be halted by a heavy hand on her shoulder.

"And where the fuck do you think you're going?"

Picking up the wrecked garment, Mindy waved it in front of Gladys in justification, pleading, "Momma, that bitch ruined all my lingerie."

"Well, it serves ya right. Ya shouldn't have fucked with her in the first place."

"And that's the other thing, Momma. Roberta's crazy in the head," Mindy exclaimed, pointing to her temple to emphasize her diagnosis. "Even the simplest joke sets her off. For everybody's sake, you need to kick her out."

Gladys withdrew a roll of cash from the pocket of her jeans. The majority of it, the result of Bobbi Jo's singing performance.

She peeled off a few bills, and offered them to Mindy. "Go buy yourself new ones. Your old ones were getting ratty anyway."

"But, Momma—"

Adding a few more, Gladys reiterated, sternly, "Go now, Mindy, before I change my mind and sell your ass to one of the houses on the Eastside."

Turning ghostly white at the thought, Mindy snatched the money and disappeared.

Left with a sobbing Bobbi Jo, Gladys said, "I don't know what your story is or where your anger comes from, nor do I care. As for today, you officially have a day off."

She handed her the rest of the cash. "Get drunk...get laid, either way, I don't want to see hide nor hair of ya 'til morning."

Bobbi Jo was not daft enough to argue. She nodded, accepted the money and began cleaning up the mess.

"Leave it. I have a houseful of women who need to learn to do something other than incite a riot.

"Oh, and remember this," Gladys cautioned. "If I ever catch you even thinking about damaging any of my merchandise, you're gonna discover the meaning of getting your ass handed to you.

"And if you're lucky, they'll find the bits and pieces of you before the river sweeps them down to the Gulf and out to sea."

Without another word, Gladys left the laundry room. Stomping up the stairs, she summoned the others, "House meeting, now."

Gathering herself, Bobbi Jo retreated to her improvised bedroom to prepare for a day out.

After an afternoon's shopping and treating herself to dinner, Bobbi Jo took in a double feature but, fearful Mindy would succeed in getting her banned from the house, could not focus on either movie.

The house had other things to concern itself with the following morning.

Bobbi Jo rose earlier than usual to prepare a special breakfast as a peace offering for her eight housemates. She went all out, pancakes, eggs, bacon, and coffee.

Laying the spread on the table, she was concerned when none of the others swarmed down the stairs as usual, impelling her to do something she had never done before. She walked to the foot of the staircase and bawled, "Breakfast."

Several minutes ticked by and one by one the tenants traipsed into the kitchen, bringing with them a heavy silence.

The last to join them was Judy, Eve's roommate.

The chair usually reserved for Eve remained empty. Bobbi Jo noticed the others glancing at it, but they said nothing.

This was so unlike the normal raucous rattle of silverware and idle conversation that Bobbi Jo blurted out, "Is Eve still asleep or something? Does she expect me to take her sorry ass breakfast in—"

"Roberta, stop," Judy dropped her fork and bolted from the room.

As Judy's footsteps faded, Alice said softly, "Good job, Roberta. The ambulance took Eve to the hospital last night." Her eyes fixed on her plate, Alice lost her appetite as well.

Feeling terrible for not being there to help, Bobbi Jo

slumped into Judy's chair. "Oh, God, I'm sorry. I had no idea."

"Nothing you could have done, Roberta," Gladys said as she entered from the back door. "Can you make me a cup of coffee, please?"

Gladys sat down and buried her head in her hands. It had been a long night and today was shaping up to be equally interminable.

The aroma of freshly brewed coffee jerked her from her reverie. Looking up, she thanked Bobbi Jo who asked, "What happened?"

Another moment of silence, then Mindy spoke, "One of her customers beat her up really badly."

"And after she took pity on the creep," Alice chimed in.

"It's my fault for letting them in," Gladys said remorsefully.

"Momma, you had no idea those guys would be so unruly," Alice tried to console her boss.

"Tell that to Eve...if she ever comes out of her coma."

"Why did he beat her up?" Bobbi Jo pressed.

It was Mindy who provided an insightful observation, "Who the hell knows. Some guys just like to use us as punching bags to get their jollies."

"Maybe she pissed him off with a crack about his missing finger," Alice joked.

"Missing finger?" Bobbi Jo's ears pricked up.

"Yeah, the ring finger on his left hand," Alice replied. "I'm guessing a jealous wife caught her man screwing around and snatched his wedding ring...finger and all."

"No," Mindy broke in. "I overheard the guy telling Eve he lost it in Korea, saving his entire unit by grabbing a North Korean grenade before it detonated. Mind, I can't figure out how it could only blow off one finger...especially that one, surely it would have damaged his whole hand.

"Either way, I'm guessing he was just playing on Eve's sympathies. She's too much of a soft touch for her own good."

"Shut it, Mindy," Gladys interjected abruptly.

"Momma?" Bobbi Jo's interest was piqued at the description of Eve's assailant. "Have these guys been here before?"

"Not all of them, but yeah, a couple have," Gladys admitted. "That's why I let them in. I assume the rest of them work for the same shipping company on the river. Why do you ask?"

"No reason in particular," Bobbi Jo lied.

"Well in any case, if y'all will excuse me. I've got things I need to do before the police chief gets here. Roberta, please show him to my office when he arrives."

"Yes, Momma."

"And we're gonna close down for a few days until the dust settles. Maybe y'all can look in on Eve in the meantime."

Heads around the table responded with a quiet nod. Each thinking, but for the grace of God, they could have very well been in Eve's place.

As for Gladys, she knew the interview with the chief would be uncomfortable. He did not like trouble from the houses in his city. It made for bad press, especially during an election year.

Unfortunately, she did not have all the answers to the questions she expected him to ask. Doubtless, his visit would conclude with Gladys bent over her desk, offering herself to the greasy old pervert.

Worse, she would end up paying for the *pleasure*...with

a tidy bundle of President Jacksons and President Grants to ensure he did not decide to close her down for an obscure housing violation.

Bobbi Jo decided it was time to bury the hatchet with Mindy, and find out more about their mysterious guest from last night.

Chapter Seven

Bobbi Jo finished cleaning the kitchen before she ventured to the upper floor. There was an unspoken rule banning her from upstairs, save the need to put out a fire.

At the foot of the staircase, she was met by most of her housemates coming down, although Mindy was not among them.

Judy was the first to reach the bottom step. Her gaze lowered, she nearly bumped into Bobbi Jo, but refused to acknowledge her as she crossed the hall to the door.

Spotting the concerned look on the housekeeper's face, Alice stopped long enough to say, "We're going to the hospital." Glancing at the front door, which Judy had left open, she added, "Don't worry about her. She knows you like Eve and had no way of knowing what happened. I guess finding your roommate in a pool of blood will screw with your head."

Bobbi Jo swallowed a scoff at this. *If anybody should know how much a bloody body can screw you up, doll, it's me.*

Instead of replying, Bobbi Jo nodded her agreement.

"She'll come around soon enough, Roberta."

Ruby hooked her arm through Alice's.

"Come on, roomie. You know how crabby Judy gets if she has to sit in the car too long."

A light bulb went off in Ruby's head, registering that no one had asked Roberta. "You wanna come with us? We're planning to grab a bite afterwards."

"Jesus Christ, Ruby, use your goddamned brain. We're not going on a picnic ya know. Show a little sympathy for Eve why dontcha," Alice lectured her friend.

Bobbi Jo shook her head, begging off the invite. "It's okay you all go ahead. Momma has me doing a bunch of chores today, so I'll go this evening."

"Have it your way, hun," Ruby said with a smile, before tugging on Alice's arm, ushering her out.

Bobbi Jo called after them, "Isn't Mindy going with you?"

"Nah." Ruby didn't look back, "said she was too tired or something. Never can tell with that one."

The heavy door thudded shut, leaving Bobbi Jo alone in the foyer. Glancing up the stairs, she decided, before she barged in on Mindy, to employ one or two of the tactics she had learned from listening to Westerns on the radio.

Saying aloud, "Never go into hostile territory without carrying a peace pipe."

Carrying the silver serving tray carefully, Bobbi Jo climbed the stairs. Understandably, no one had eaten much of her massive spread this morning, so she thought a little surprise for Mindy might be welcomed.

Mindy's room, at the top of the stairs — and probably at one time, the master bedroom — was a tacit declaration of her status as a moneymaker for Gladys. Mindy had also earned the right to forego a roommate. The only one afforded such luxury.

Balancing the tray on her upturned palm, Bobbi Jo knocked on the door.

She pressed her ear against one of the panels only to catch a sigh and the sound of approaching footsteps.

"Just a sec," Mindy sang out.

"It's me, Mindy," Bobbi Jo called back.

The steps came to a halt.

"Go away, Roberta. I've neither the energy nor the mood to deal with your shit this morning."

"It's nothing like that, Mindy. I come in peace...bearing gifts."

The door swung open slowly to reveal a woman clad in nothing but an Oriental robe, the sash untied. At first Bobbi Jo thought Mindy had done so on purpose for the shock factor, but the latter's tired, red-rimmed eyes convinced her otherwise.

Unable to help herself, Bobbi Jo gave the exposed portions of Mindy's body a once over. While the other woman's features no doubt enchanted the opposite sex, a closer examination in the light of day, told a story of a girl whose entry into womanhood had been less than pleasurable.

Traces of bruising, at the awful yellow stage marred her breasts, and Bobbi Jo assumed she must have used ridiculous amounts of concealer to hide them.

Mindy took a drag from her cigarette and blew it ceiling-ward from the side of her mouth. "So what did I do to deserve you daring to enter our domain, let alone with a silver platter?"

"I figured with everything that's been going on today, you and me should try a do-over. I know we didn't start out on the right foot."

Mindy waved Bobby Jo in, and although the invite felt steeped in sarcasm, Bobbi Jo didn't let it get to her. She was under no illusion that they would ever be drinking buddies.

As Mindy turned away from the door, Bobby Jo thought she saw scars caused by cigarettes on her thighs. Gladys's threat about selling Mindy to the Eastside made more sense. Bobbi Jo surmised that was where she had started out.

"Well, don't just stand there, come in," Mindy said. "You'll have to forgive me if I dress while we share this heart-to-heart. Since Momma has us closed I've got..."

Bobbi Jo placed the tray on a small table wedged between two wingback chairs along the wall. Making herself comfortable in one, she took stock of the room.

It was a far cry from where she or others slept. It made her wonder what Gladys's room looked like. Another room off limits to Bobbi Jo, which was fine with her because it was less work to tackle.

She tossed in an occasional *Mhm* to whatever Mindy was prattling on about.

"...and then I plan on setting myself on fire and jumping into the Mississippi,"

Mindy stopped digging through her closet, the unexpected silence brought Bobbi Jo back to the conversation. "Oh, that sounds fun," she replied. "Need any help?"

Mindy glared at her guest. Her expression informing Bobbi Jo, the jig was up.

"Okay, Roberta, 'fess up. What are you up to, other than offering to help me kill myself?"

Bobbi Jo offered Mindy one of the cups of coffee as a ploy to get her to take the chair opposite.

The lure succeeded. As much as Mindy would love her rival to fall off the face of the Earth, she loved her coffee more, and accepted the drink.

"Okay, girl, you have five minutes." Mindy tapped the clock on the table.

Taking a sip of the heady brew for courage, Bobbi Jo said, "I want to know more about what happened last night...especially about the guy who beat up Eve."

"Once again, why? Eve is no more or less friendly to you than anybody else, so why do you care?"

"That's a pretty crass—"

"Stow it."

"Let me just say...I may have history with him...I need to know for sure."

Interested in finding out anything about the mysterious Roberta's back story, Mindy chose a Danish from the pile, Bobbi Jo had generously heaped on the tray, and made herself comfortable.

Bobbi Jo realized gaining anything from Mindy was going to require a concession on her part. Gulping a fortifying mouthful, she shared the story of the day at Donner Pass.

By the end, her lips were quivering. Images she had spent years repressing, rearing up in her mind as though it was yesterday. Bobbi Jo willed them to drown in the ripples of her coffee.

It was then, Bobbi Jo warned herself to save the gory details of her life afterwards. *No sense boring her or giving her more information to use against me.*

The look on Mindy's face was anything but bored. She squawked in astonishment, "They murdered your family in front of you?"

She nodded, but clarified, "Well, only my dad, but my mom's screams..." Bobbi Jo paused when she felt Mindy's hand press her knee. She could see tears in Mindy's eyes. While she wanted to know more of Mindy's life as well, this was not the time.

"Oh my God, and I invited him into the house?" Mindy recoiled in horror at what she let slip.

"Huh? I thought Momma opened the door? That's what she said in the kitchen."

Rising from her chair, Mindy paced fretfully about the room. Her pale face contorted, a turmoil of conscience raging behind her amber-flecked eyes.

"You have to swear you won't tell Momma, Roberta."

"Tell her what, Mindy? What exactly did you do?"

"I invited those guys over...well, Mitch at least...he brought the rest of them."

"Who's Mitch?"

"My b-boyfriend," Mindy admitted. Having a relationship was not expressly prohibited by Momma, but she frowned on it, arguing that mixing business with love was a recipe for disaster.

"So your boyfriend knows you sleep with other guys... for money no less?" For the life of her, Bobbi Jo could not prevent the judgment in her tone.

"Well, he pays too...sometimes."

"Whatever," Bobbi Jo sniped, her empathy for Mindy dwindling. "Tell me more about his friend, like what his name is and where I can find him."

"I don't know anything more than he works at the docks

on the river with Mitch and the other guys. D-do you think Gladys will kick me out of the house?"

"I have no idea," Bobbi Jo replied as she rose to collect the tray. "But if I were you, I'd have a conversation with her before she finds out on her own."

As Bobbi Jo left the room, she heard Mindy implore, "Please, keep quiet and don't cause any problems. It can't be the same guy. Just let it go."

"Can't," was all Bobbi Jo said, as she closed the door. The sound of something shattering against it, a good indication that she probably had one less cup to wash.

Happy with the information she had just gained, Bobbi Jo descended the stairs, reaching the bottom in time to hear the chime of the doorbell.

Steadying the tray against her waist, she opened the door with her free hand.

There, puffed and stuffed in his uniform, stood Chief of Police Walter Owens. He gave the girl a lecherous grin which sent a chill down Bobbi Jo's spin and made her want to retch violently.

"Good morning, my dear." He undressed her with his eyes. "Is your employer at home?"

Suppressing a burning desire to hit the man upside the head with the tray, Bobbi Jo gave an impish smirk. "Yes, sir, my Mistress told me to expect you. Please follow me to her office?" She turned to lead him into the house, but the thought of him following her left her uneasy.

Spinning around, she held out the silver tray. "I beg you, sir, this tray is awfully heavy for someone like me, and I can tell by your stature it would be of little effort for you. May I impose on you? I'm sure the Mistress will reward you for your kindness."

Bobbi Jo kept her eyes lowered in a demure manner, and added a soft whimper for effect.

While the Police Chief was the epitome of a misogynist, the opportunity of scoring points with Gladys as well as this lovely young thing could not be ignored. Lifting the tray from the girl's grasp, he fell into step behind her.

He arched a brow. "Why is there only one cup on the tray?"

Bobbi Jo realized in addition to having its mate smashed to bits, the remaining cup was one she had drunk from in Mindy's bedroom.

Clearing her throat, she lied, "Mistress thought you would appreciate a cup *specially sweetened* by one of her girls."

Reaching Gladys's office door, she opened it and stepped to the side to allow him to pass. She waited for Gladys to greet the Police Chief before she shut the door behind him.

Bobbi Jo felt sorry for her employer, but chalked up what was about to occur as the cost of doing business.

Unfastening her apron, she dropped it on the counter on her way out of the back door.

The DeSoto rolled up to the entrance of the Longshoremen's Association local hall. Bobbi Jo sat behind the wheel studying the building as she plotted her next move.

She watched as men wandered in and out of the hall. Some clutching documents, she assumed to be work assignments, others looked as though they were stuffing envelopes into their pockets.

Women descended like vultures. In the manner of Times Square pickpockets, they retrieved the goods the men had unsuccessfully tried to conceal, with practiced ease.

Their attire told Bobbi Jo, the women were not professionals, and the disgruntled expressions of the men confirmed these were wives and girlfriends...and this was payday.

The scene gave Bobbi Jo an idea. All she needed was a small cushion.

Bursting into the building, she made sure the door banged open with the correct intensity.

With all the indignation she could muster, she demanded, "Where is he? Where is the bastard?" She was now the focal point of everyone in the room. "I know you're hiding his sorry ass here somewhere. I want to see him now."

The shop steward bolted up from his desk. Hysterical women were never good for the morale of his union members.

"Ma'am, please control yourself," he begged gruffly, pulling the cigar butt from his mouth, and belching a cloud of smoke, which billowed around him.

"Why the hell should I...?" She took a step closer to the man, shouting in his face, "And who are you to tell me what I should be doing, anyway?"

As was his habit when confronted with a difficult situation, he waved his cigar as though creating a smoke screen to vanish behind magically. "The name is Granger, ma'am. I'm the shop steward and I must insist you—" he began.

Evidently, the woman was not about to fall for his tricks.

"So, are you in on it too, Granger ma'am?" Bobbi Jo was giving the performance of her life.

"It's just Granger, miss, and what are you talking about? In on what?"

"Protecting that good for nothing who got me pregnant and refuses to take responsibility. He's paying you to hide him isn't he."

"Miss, I can assure you the Brotherhood is not in the business of getting involved with the personal lives of our members."

"I knew you'd cover for him. Just remember, the next time I come, it will be with TV cameras and the press and you can explain to them how you run your shop."

Bobbi Jo dabbed her fake tears with a handkerchief. "How can you be so heartless? At least let me talk to him."

The last thing Granger wanted was reporters congregating in his hall, no matter the reason.

Ushering the woman to his desk, Granger circled around to the opposite side. The old rolling chair squealed its disapproval at being required to support the man's rotund frame.

Granger withdrew the thick membership book from his drawer and thumbed through it. Getting to the list of names, addresses, and work assignments, he said politely, "Look, how about you tell me who you're looking for and I'll see whether I can find him for you."

His question shook Bobbi Jo. While she had heard his name repeated in the house that night...a name forever burned in her memory...she only knew Roy's given name. It was only Buchanan's she knew in full.

It was too late to turn back now.

"His name is Roy."

Granger raised his head in astonishment. "Roy what? Look, young lady, you're gonna have to give me something more to go on."

"What?" Bobbi Jo asked, annoyed that Granger expected her to provide more than the man's first name. "How many asses named Roy could you possibly have working on these run down docks?"

"Look, I don't have all day to waste on you—"

Bobbi Jo clutched her 'swollen' stomach, wailing, "Oh my God, the baby just kicked. My daughter is just as upset as I am."

She figured declaring the imaginary child to be a girl would add an extra tug to the man's heartstrings. If one hysterical female was enough to contend with, *two* ought to be more than he could handle.

On the contrary, Granger was losing patience with the whole matter. "If you don't know the last name of the guy you were sleeping around with, might you at least tell me what he looks like?" he jeered.

Her arms continuing to cradle her nonexistent baby, Bobbi Jo gave him the only identifying mark she could. "He's missing his ring finger. On his left hand. War wound."

Granger canted his head at the description.

Bobbi Jo noted his expression. "Is there a problem?" Throwing herself back into hysterics, she wailed, "Oh, No. He lied to me about working here as well?"

Shutting his book with a snap, Granger stood and escorted the woman to the door with a beefy arm. "You and your kid would be best served staying away from that reprobate, especially since he couldn't be bothered to give you his real name."

"What do you mean? It isn't Roy?"

"Hardly...his name is Phil Danvers. Sorriest drunk I know. Take my advice. Go home, have your baby and leave the likes of Phil Danvers well alone."

Pushing Bobbi Jo out of the hall, Granger threw after her, "And if you have any brains, which hooking up with Danvers in the first place tells me you don't, you'll give it up for adoption."

Chapter Eight

The stench of stale cigarettes and spilled beer permeated Bobbi Jo's soul. While she had grown immune to the cheap perfume the women of the house doused themselves in, night after night, she worried she would never rid herself of this rancid aroma.

To make matters worse, the late afternoon drizzle added a layer of wet dog to her overly sensitive nose as she dashed from her car to the entrance of the third dockside dive of the day. Pushing through the door, Bobbi Jo walked across to the bar and a waiting stool.

Lighting a smoke, a habit she had picked up from her time at Gladys's, Bobbi Jo twirled the stool around to scrutinize the patrons.

The place itself was no different from any of the other joints. The people were all hard and calloused, drinking themselves into a stupor as quickly as they could before they either went home...or to work.

The sound of two guys shooting pool in the corner garnered Bobbi Jo's curiosity. As her eyes adjusted to the gloom she made out their faces, determining neither man was whom she sought.

Still, having an attractive young thing looking in their direction, prompted the one waiting for his shot to stroll over to where she was sitting.

"Bud, get me another beer, and my lady friend whatever she wants." He winked at Bobbi Jo before reminding the barman, "and make sure to put them on my tab."

The guy figured it would impress the girl to know he was important enough in the establishment to charge it.

That was until Bud stepped up with two bottles of beer. "Eight bits, Earl, and your tab is long past due."

"My man, you must be mistaken, but we'll save that conversation for another time."

He turned his attention to Bobbi Jo.

She side-eyed her new *friend* as she picked up the cold bottle and took a sip. It had surprised her how easy it was to get served in these places. No one bothered to card the seventeen-year-old, and there had been no lack of men willing to ply her with alcohol, hoping to extend their...acquaintance.

All of which she declined because they failed to provide her with the information, she had spent hours searching for.

"What brings a sexy thing like you into this dump... besides brightening up my night, of course?"

Bobbi Jo took another drink. The door opened, drawing her gaze to the mirror behind the bar long enough to study the couple who entered. For split-second, she locked eyes with the woman via the reflection.

She watched the woman shimmy against the man, casually, like a cat marking its territory. A subtle gesture, but one Bobbi Jo recognized immediately. She had seen the women in the house employ the same tactic when they decided which prospective customer to entice upstairs. A clear warning to the others to back off.

Raising the bottle to the mirror, Bobbi Jo toasted the woman who directed her *date* to the rear of the bar.

Once again, the pool player tried to strike up a conversation. "Do you shoot pool?"

Smirking, Bobbi Jo turned to him. "By the looks of it, only your friend there does."

"Bah, Luke's just on a lucky streak this game. Been kicking his ass all night otherwise."

"Maybe I should go talk to him then," Bobbi Jo taunted.

"How can you be so cruel...after I bought you a beer and all. At least give me a name. Only the right thing to do."

"Okay," Bobbi Jo agreed. She leaned close to Earl's ear, letting her warm breath tease his ear. "Philip Danvers. Know where I can find him?"

The mere mention of the name made Earl recoil. "Look, I don't want any trouble with him. You should have told me you were his woman in the first place."

"What makes you think I belong to him?"

"Why else would you be looking for him?"

"Let's just say I have business with him. Is that a good enough reason?"

"You a cop or something?"

Draining the rest of the bottle, Bobbi Jo thumped it on the bar as she set it down. "Do I look like a cop?"

"Nowadays who can tell?"

Luke shouted across the bar, "Stop trying to get laid and cough up the ten spot you just lost."

Bobbi Jo murmured, "Make ya a bet. If I beat Luke there, you don't have to pay him...but you tell me everything you know about Danvers."

"And if you lose?"

"I'll cover both bets...and you can take me home."

Earl stared at her in disbelief. "You mean as in—"

Bobbi Jo nodded, stealing his beer and his pool cue. Sauntering across the floor, she cooed over her shoulder. "Coming?"

Reaching the pool table, Bobbi Jo brushed aside the quarter already there for the next game, digging another out of her pocket. With a flip from her thumb, she sent it tumbling toward Luke.

"Next game is you and me," she said, setting Earl's bottle on the edge of the table.

"Hey now, little lady," Luke objected. "I don't believe in taking advantage of a woman, even a stupid one."

"Is that another way of saying you're afraid to get shown up by one?" Bobbi Jo chalked her cue as Luke dithered.

Walking to the coin slot, she guided his hand down, urging him to release the quarter.

Their interaction had stirred the interest of the patrons who congregated closer to the table.

This left Luke with little choice but to accept the challenge. Figuratively, he owned this table, no one in the bar had ever beaten him. His ego refused to allow this wisp of a girl to embarrass him in front of the others.

Dropping the quarter into the slot, he pushed the lever in, unleashing the balls. He racked them up, saying to Bobbi Jo, "I'll go easy on ya, dime a ball."

"Chump change. Double or nothing on this one's bet," she said, jerking a thumb toward Earl.

"Come on, girl, that's a lot of money for somebody like you to be carrying around."

Bobbi Jo knew it was dumb thing to do, but she pulled a twenty from her pocket and laid it on the side of the table.

"Happy?"

Luke shrugged. "Your loss. Go ahead and break. You might as well get one shot in. Oh, and remember to call your shots."

With the cue ball in place, Bobbi Jo bent over the table edge, earning more than a few whistles of approval from the crowd, and slid the cue along her thumb and knuckle of her index finger.

The cue ball jolted forward, ricocheting the one-ball off the side of the eight and into the corner pocket. The remaining balls disbursed neatly about the green felt. The backspin she delivered at the base of the white ball left it exactly where she wanted it.

The two-ball lay close to the right side pocket, giving her an easy shot, and setting herself up for the three. As she lined up the shot, she smiled sweetly at Luke, who was grimacing.

Sinking the three, she turned to the four perched behind the five along the back rail near the opposite corner pocket.

As she studied the positions, a snicker rumbled through the crowd who realized what she was contemplating.

Luke thought she was crazy as well, and began chalking his cue. A renewed confidence welled up convincing him, he would get his chance to run the table and show the bitch up, after she missed.

"Did I tell you about the night I spent shooting pool with Willie Mosconi? When they say he's an amazing trick shot..." Bobbi Jo struck the cue ball hard, propelling it at the four.

The impact caused the four to leap over the five and into the pocket, the cue rolling to a gentle rest against the five.

"...it's a disservice to the man. He's a wizard plain and simple."

The shot elicited hoots and applause from the spectators. Watching her coax the five into the pocket, felt anti-climactic.

As Bobbi Jo angled her body to send the six-ball into the far corner, a pool cue was thwacked down onto the table making her jump. Twisting, she saw Luke standing next to her, empty-handed.

"What gives, man?" she asked.

"I know when I'm being hustled, bitch. Just take your goddamned money and get the hell out of here."

The round of boos at Luke's forfeit nearly drowned out his threat to Earl who was scooping up the cash.

"If I catch either of you in this bar again, I'll kill the both of ya."

Tipping the brim of his greasy cap, Earl groused, "Sore loser."

Earl turned to find Bobbi Jo behind him, her hand out. Grabbing it, he led her out into the murky parking lot.

Reaching the passenger side of his truck, he smiled and stuffed the bill into his pocket. "Never let it be said, I am not a man of my word. I'll be more than happy to escort you to where you should be able to find Danvers, though I still can't figure out why you want him."

"Thanks, but I have my own vehicle and, as for why, I need to pay him back for something."

"You sure I can't just take you to a couple of bars I know instead? We could clean up tonight at the tables...and well, I make a mean breakfast."

"As tempting as that sounds..." Bobbi Jo replied, rising up on her tiptoes to kiss the man on the cheek, and retrieve her twenty from his pocket, "...I'll take a raincheck on the breakfast. Now about that address?"

The DeSoto stopped in front of a rundown shack at the edge of the dockyard. The weather had seen fit to upgrade itself from a light shower to a torrential downpour. Flashes of lightning framed the small house, giving it an ominous vibe.

Alighting, Bobbi Jo paused, pondering her next move. She had no gun and, from what she had learned of Danvers, he was not one to be trifled with. An even more sickening thought hit her.

What if this isn't even the guy I'm looking for? What if it is just a bizarre coincidence?

Through the thunder, a female voice whispered in her ear, "You know you're right, Bobbi Jo."

She scanned her surrounds but she was alone. Shaking her head, she studied the house again.

It's not worth it, she argued with herself. *You just need to get back into your car and carry your sorry butt home.*

Reaching for the handle, another crack of lightning streaked downward, freezing Bobbi Jo in place.

The woman's cry replaced the thunder, "You need to avenge us."

This time, Bobbi Jo thought she recognized the voice. "*Momma?*" her tone incredulous.

"Yes, poppet. I'm here. Please...please do what the police refused to do. Serve this miserable excuse of a human the justice he thought he would never have to face."

"B-but how, Momma?"

Bobbi Jo gasped when the trunk latch on the DeSoto released, the interior light flickering as gusts of wind toyed with the lid. She crept closer and raised it, exposing the tire iron lying on the spare.

"Do it, sweetheart. Pick it up and use it," the invisible speaker urged.

Hesitant fingers wrapped around the metal bar. Closing the trunk, she hunched her shoulders against the sheets of rain and trudged to the house.

"That's it, Bobbi Jo. Keep going," her mother's voice drove her on. "You're almost at the porch, just a few more steps."

She approached the front door, the click of her shoes on the worn wooden boards sounded overly loud. As though someone else was controlling her body, she watched her hand lift to knock on the glass.

She listened to the thud of heavy boots crossing the room at the other side of the door. Light from the sole fixture, missing any decorative globe, flooded the porch. Bobbi Jo hid the tire iron behind her.

"Who the fuck's out there?" The demand definitely came from a disgruntled male.

Drenched by the rain, hair plastered to her scalp, and silhouetted by jagged flashes of lightning, Bobbi Jo resembled the Angel of Death.

"What'er yer sellin', I ain't buyin'."

"Mr. Danvers. I work for the union hall. Mr. Granger sent me because we screwed up your pay," Bobbi Jo lied, her mother's voice feeding her the words.

"What the hell?" Danvers barked. "Since when did Granger give a shit about being right with the pay?"

"I'm not sure, Mr. Danvers. All I know is he sent me out

to give you what you're due. Can you open up so I can get home?"

"Jesus Christ," Danvers reply was testy as he unlocked the door. "Feds are probably comin' to town to check his books. Would serve him right to end up in jail for cookin' 'em. Stupid bastard."

Stepping onto the porch, he glared at Bobbi Jo.

She studied his face. It looked older than his age warranted, but his eyes, though bloodshot and bleary from years of hard living, were the same eyes she recalled from the night he spent howling in her kitchen while her momma tried to treat his hand.

His hand!

Bobbi Jo's examination lowered to study his hand, outstretched to receive the unexpected bonus. Missing was the third finger. The scar that remained, reminiscent of her mother's cross-stitch.

"Well, girl, I ain't got all night."

"You have that right, *Roy*."

In one fluid movement, Bobby Jo hoisted the tire iron over her head. Danvers's mouth opened, but Bobbi Jo did not hear what he said, as she concentrated all her strength on the downswing, picturing Danvers's skull splintering, brains and blood spraying in all directions.

Instead of the crunch of iron on bone, pain ratcheted through her forearm, and the clatter was that of the tire iron landing on the porch. Danvers had blocked the attack.

She leveled her gaze at him in time to see his fist hurl toward her jaw. The jab sent her tumbling backward into the mud.

"Who the fuck do you think you are, little girl? Bigger men than you have tried to take me out and failed."

Rubbing her jaw, she shrieked, "Where are the others?"

"What others? Santy Claus and the Easter Bunny?"

"You know damn well who I'm talking about. Buchanan and the other two."

Roy roared with laughter. "How the fuck would I know? Last I heard, the brothers were in an oil field in Oklahoma...or jail. Can't remember which."

"And Buchanan?"

"Wish I fucking knew...he still owes me money, not that it's any of your concern."

Snatching the iron from the porch, he approached her menacingly, tapping the bar against the palm of his hand.

"Seems only fair to teach ya how to kill a man proper like with one of these, since ya did such a pathetic job just now. Mind, I don't figure you'll remember much of it when I'm done with ya."

Bobbi Jo did not move, nor did she beg for mercy. She watched with macabre interest as Danvers swung the rod aloft to deliver the death blow.

An unexpected flash blinded her, and the hair on her arms stood on end. She heard an agonized howl, followed by a noxious odor — like a blend of scorched barbeque and ozone.

As her vision cleared, she saw the charred remains of Phil Danvers, spread-eagled on the ground, the tire iron steaming under the rain.

Closer inspection revealed his boots had been blown off, holes burned through the soles.

"Serves ya right, you bastard, but I'd have preferred to see you getting zapped in the electric chair."

"Quit dallying, Bobbi Jo," the voice chided. "You need to check his house. There might be a clue as to where the rest of the scum are."

Gingerly, her sleeve wrapped around her hand, Bobbi

Jo ensured the makeshift weapon had lost its charge and wasn't going to cause third-degree burns.

Picking it up, she said to the corpse, "Best to be prepared. God knows who or what else might be waiting for me in there."

She used the end of the iron to open the door. The furnishings looked and smelled as though Danvers had stolen them from a church donation center.

The house lacked carpet, which made the black and white television all the louder. The walls were devoid of any art, save a couple of pictures of the man, she had known as Roy, in uniform.

Tiptoeing through the living room, Bobbi Jo avoided touching anything.

"If anybody cares enough to come looking for ya, Roy, there's no sense giving the cops any more evidence than necessary. It's bad enough that too many people might remember me asking about ya."

In front of the television, on a small table alongside an armchair, she discovered a pile of discarded mail. Placing the iron on the table and, keeping the sleeve over her fingers, she searched through it.

At the bottom of the stack, Bobbi Jo came across an unopened letter from the Oklahoma State Penitentiary. She stuffed it in her pocket without bothering to verify the name. It was enough of a clue by itself.

Latching the door, she descended from the porch and into the pouring rain, glancing in satisfaction at Danvers, tendrils of smoke still rising from his singed corpse.

Opening the car door, she tossed the implement of her justice onto the passenger side floor. Once behind the wheel, she sat for a moment and stared at the rain.

"You made me proud, dear," Bobbi Jo heard her mother say.

Without answering, she started the DeSoto, ground it into gear, and drove away.

Gladys heard noises coming from the butler's pantry. At this time of the morning, she was concerned they had an uninvited guest in the house. Clutching her .25 caliber, she tiptoed across the kitchen.

Her thumb slid the hammer back as she peeked into the room where she saw Bobbi Jo packing hastily. Carefully, Gladys uncocked the *mouse gun* and tucked it into her robe pocket.

She cleared her throat. "Leaving so soon, Roberta?"

Startled, Bobbi Jo spun around to see her employer standing in the doorway.

"Unfortunately, some stuff has cropped up that I need to take care of."

"Pity." Gladys lit a cigarette. Exhaling a cloud of smoke, she said, "I was getting used to you being around here. Any chance of you coming back this way when you're finished with whatever it is that's got you in a tizzy?"

"Highly unlikely, but you never know."

"Well, either way, wait there a second before you rush off."

Gladys vanished to return with something in her hand. "It's bad enough you're not giving me two weeks' notice. I figure I'm not gonna get a forwarding address either, so you might as well take your pay with you."

She held out an envelope. "Take it and don't argue."

Bobbi Jo did as instructed, noting it was thicker than it ought to have been. "Momma, I-I can't take all of this."

Waving aside the girl's protest, Gladys disappeared into the darkness of the house, quipping, "Consider it a bribe to bring ya back. And if that doesn't work, consider it an investment in your future. Now get out of here before I put your ass to work upstairs."

Chapter Nine

Oklahoma

Dawn saw the deluge subside and rays of the morning sun peek through the clouds.

After battling to keep the DeSoto on the highway for hours, Bobbi Jo clicked her wipers onto low as she crossed the Missouri-Oklahoma state line, finally able to see the road clearly.

Exhaustion, accompanied by hunger, swamped her, but she was determined to push through to Oklahoma City. Turning the radio up, she listened to the news through the static, thankful not to hear mention of a torched body being discovered in St Louis.

A few miles outside the city, Bobbi Jo came across a quaint motor inn. Its ten cabins were set neatly around the semi-circle of the drive. An old Bur Oak sat prominently in the middle, its branches spreading out in all directions, providing inviting shade.

Pulling up to the office, Bobbi Jo alighted, pausing to eyeball the vehicles parked in front of a handful of the cabins. Although positive, she would not see a Highway Patrol car, it was a relief to have her assumption confirmed.

She strolled into the office hoping to book either cabin five or six where she was less likely to be seen from the road...should anyone be on the hunt for her DeSoto.

"Hello," the overly chirpy greeting from the young woman sitting behind the counter was embellished with a saccharine beam which seemed to split her face from ear to ear.

Bobbi Jo quelled an uncharitable desire to slap the smile right off the receptionist, and managed a genial, "Good morning. Do you happen to have anything available for tonight and perhaps a longer stay?"

"You're in luck, sweetie. We have a couple. Seven and ten, though I'd recommend ten, cuz it's just been freshly painted and has a queen bed. It's really cute and cheery, especially if you're intending to spend some time with us."

"If it's okay, I'll take seven. Hopin' there will be less road noise."

The woman cocked her head, a trifle miffed at failing to rent the more expensive cabin. "Your loss. How long do you think you might be here?"

"Let's start with a week, and go from there."

"A week? That'll be $49, in advance."

Eyeing Bobbi Jo while she fished out the cash Gladys had given her, the woman sniped, "That isn't too much for you is it? This isn't the Y after all."

Bobbi Jo threw a crumpled fifty on the counter. "I believe this should cover it."

The clerk fetched the key from its slot. About to pass it over, she withdrew her hand.

"Are your parents traveling with you?" Her tone, accusatory.

"Do I look like I need a chaperone?"

"As a matter of fact...yes. Can I see some ID? I don't need to be harboring runaways."

"Oh, for Christ's sake." Bobbi Jo pawed through her purse for a nonexistent ID proving she was over twenty-one. "Ya know what, lady, I don't have time for your stupid games. Just give me back my money and keep your key. I'll go to the next place."

The end of the vacation season loomed, and fewer tourists required lodgings.

Against her better judgment, the receptionist relented. "Let's not be hasty. Just know I'll be watching you closely. I will not tolerate any gentlemen in your cabin. We don't run that kinda place here."

"If I find out you're trying to sneak someone into your cabin without my knowledge, I will kick your ass out without a refund, and *don't* think I won't hesitate to report you to the police. We are a family-friendly resort. I intend to keep it that way."

"Yeah, yeah," Bobbi Jo swiped the key as the woman offered it once more. "I promise not to sully the venerable reputation of the..." she paused to look at the room key for the name, "...Hodge Podge Motor Lodge."

"See you don't."

Bobbi Jo dropped the key in her purse and remembered she was due change. Holding out her hand, she reminded the clerk, "I believe you owe me a dollar."

"Consider it a security deposit, in case of damages."

Too tired to continue the fight...or drive on, Bobbi Jo was on the verge of flipping the woman the bird when she thought better of it. Contenting herself with a major eye roll, she trudged back to her car, and drove to cabin seven.

Before she took her suitcase in, she unlocked the door

and checked out the room. It had a musty smell. "Typical," she griped, and opened the windows to freshen it up.

On the dresser stood a small television set. Bobbi Jo turned it on, surprised to see it had decent reception, but when she tried to move it for a better view from the bed, realized it was bolted in place, which made her chuckle.

Now the cross breeze was dispersing the stale air, the cabin seemed less dreary and she felt she could tolerate it for a few days.

Retrieving her belongings from the car, she installed them on the case stand in the room.

The only thing she bothered to unpack was the letter she had taken from Roy's table. Sitting at the desk, she checked the postmark, noting it had been sent almost six months ago.

"Who the hell receives a letter from jail and never opens it?" Bobbi Jo queried out loud, while happy Roy had ignored it. It provided the sender's full name: Clarence Fulbright.

She was unsure what emotion knowing Clarence's last name elicited. Relief that she did not have to waste time trying to discover it or anger that he had never faced prosecution for the murder of her family.

She turned it over, and saw the tell-tale marks that the contents inside had been screened by the proper authorities before it was mailed.

Bobbi Jo searched the desk drawer for a letter opener. While the blade which slid into view looked more like a butter knife than a genuine opener, she reckoned it would do the job.

Slitting the envelope, she removed and unfolded a handwritten letter, squinting to decipher the chicken scratch.

Royboy,

It's your old buddy Clarence. I know it's been a stretch, but as you can see, I need your help. My stupid brother Daryl got himself killed when the two of us tried to stick up a liquor store. Never expected the old man behind the counter to have a shotgun.

Anyway, water under the bridge.

And about things under the bridge, neither Daryl nor me planned to leave ya like that. It was all Buchanan's doing. We never saw a cent of that venture either.

Bobbi Jo reread the line, and scoffed, "Venture, eh? Guess you can't say robbery when you're trying to get out of jail."

What I need your help with, old buddy, is to come down to McAlester to vouch for me at my parole hearing on the 27th of April.

I pray you can, cuz I need to get out of here and you're my only hope. I'll buy ya a beer and steak dinner to celebrate when you get me out. You might also be interested to hear what I've unearthed about finding Buchanan's sorry ass.

Don't let me down. I promise it is worth the trip.

Your buddy,

Clarence

Inmate No. 6002275

"Well, Clarence, it's obvious Roy never showed up and I'm happy to hear there is one less of you bastards to track down," Bobbi Jo said as she slotted the sheet back into the envelope.

"With any luck, you're languishing in the Oklahoma Penn. I guess there is only one way to find out for sure."

Lifting the telephone receiver from its cradle, Bobbi Jo dialed the front desk.

"Hodge Podge Motor Lodge, reception," the clerk

answered. "I hope you're finding everything to your liking, miss. Cabin ten is—"

"Yes, yes," Bobbi Jo interrupted. "Is it possible to dial long distance to McAlester and charge it to the room?"

"Oh, heavens no, miss. The room phones are for local calls only. Why would you want to call there anyway?"

Ignoring the question, Bobbi Jo asked patiently, "Is there anywhere I can make the call?"

"Well, there is a payphone booth up the road at the service station. I suppose you could try there."

"Fine," Bobbi Jo sighed.

"Is there anything else I can get—"

Bobbi Jo hung up on her without a second thought. Having had enough of the morning, she climbed into the bed and surrendered to the sandman.

"The Fugitive."

Bobbi Jo awoke with a start hearing the proclamation. Bolting upright, she looked around expecting to find her bed ringed with cops, service revolvers drawn.

As her brain swept away the cobwebs, she realized she was still alone in her cabin and had forgotten to turn off the television before she fell asleep.

She glanced at her watch; it was past noon. Her empty stomach had told her as much.

Straightening herself out, Bobbi Jo drove to the service station down the road, hoping there was a café connected to it.

The clerk's description of *down the road* was generous. Bobbi Jo was still on the road half an hour later, approaching the outskirts of Oklahoma City.

She thought about turning back, however, not only was she starving at this point, but also the car was running on fumes.

Luckily, she reached the service station gas pumps before the DeSoto began sputtering.

The bell cord she rolled over brought the attendant to her window.

Tipping his cap, he asked, "Fill 'er up, ma'am?"

"Please...and check the water." The radiator had not caused any problems since St Louis, but she thought it wise to make sure all the same.

"Yes, ma'am." The man went to carry out his customer's bidding.

While he tended to the vehicle, Bobbi Jo who had spotted the phone booth at the corner of the property, grabbed her purse, and walked over.

Shutting the door behind her, she spilled her coins out onto the metal ledge. For a moment, a sense of nostalgia and sorrow hit her thinking about the day she arrived on Gladys's doorstep.

Dialing o, she waited for the operator to come on the line.

"Number please?" A woman with a *Business Only* tone asked.

"Um...I'm sorry but I don't know the number, ma'am,"

Bobbi Jo replied apologetically. "I need to be connected to the Oklahoma State Penitentiary in McAlester, please."

"Any particular office, ma'am?"

"I guess the main office."

"Yes, ma'am. Please deposit a dollar and a quarter for the first three minutes."

Bobbi Jo listened to the chime and clicks radiating from the phone as she slotted in the required coinage. The line fell quiet for a moment, then the operator spoke again.

"Your party is connected, ma'am."

"Thank you," Bobbi Jo said as she was linked through to another woman.

"Oklahoma State Penitentiary. How may I help you?"

In a courteous voice, and attempting to sound older than she was, Bobbi Jo asked, "Good afternoon, ma'am. My name is Roberta Fulbright, and I'm embarrassed to ask, but I am trying to find out whether my brother, Clarence, is still an inmate at your facility. Since his incarceration, he has refused any contact with the family."

"Fulbright you say?"

"Yes, ma'am, Clarence Fulbright. I have his prison number if that is any help."

"No, that is not necessary. Please hold."

The line went silent. Bobbi Jo feared the woman might have presumed this was a prank and cut the call, but she dared not hang up.

Finally, the handset crackled back to life. "Did you find the—"

It was not the same woman. "Please deposit fifty cents for the next minute."

Grumbling, Bobbi Jo dropped in two more quarters. Picking through the dwindling stack of change, there was a distinct possibility she would run out of money before obtaining *any* information.

She heard another click, and scrabbled for more coins.

"Miss?" asked the voice on the other end.

"Yes?"

"Says here your brother was paroled in April. Good behavior."

"Do you have a present address?"

"Miss, I can hardly give something like that out over the phone."

"Please, ma'am. This is important. I need to let him know of our mother's passing."

Bobbi Jo sprinkled an adequate amount of tears and sniffles into her earnest plea.

She thought her request was going to be denied but, after a long moment, a grudging sigh echoed in her ear.

"Fine, but you did not get this from me."

"You have my word, ma'am."

The woman hesitated once more before divulging the last known address. It was somewhere in Oklahoma City.

Bobbi Jo heard a shocked gasp.

"Ma'am, it says here that Mr. Fulbright has no living relativ—"

In possession of what she needed, Bobbi Jo hung up. Opening the phone book, she located a map of metropolitan Oklahoma City, tore it out and tucked it into her purse.

Walking back to her car, she paid the attendant. "By the way, is that café across the street worth a damn?"

"Oh yes, ma'am. The missus waits tables over there. Best food this side of OKC."

Chapter Ten

Bobbi Jo took the attendant's advice and drove to the other side of the road.

The café was bustling with truckers, and vacationing families on their way to God only knew where. She stood at the door for a few moments before determining nobody was going to escort her to a table. Bobbi Jo had no qualms about seating herself, especially if it meant she could sit anywhere she wanted.

Finding a booth in the corner, she waved the more mature-looking of the two brunette waitresses to the table.

As the woman drew closer, Bobbi Jo was struck by her features. She was gifted with high cheekbones and had a cute, slight bend in her nose. Her reddish-brown skin tone masked her age well, and her coarse, dark hair had been spared any touches of gray.

Her most captivating physical trait were her almond-shaped, heavy-lidded eyes. They were a sparkling azure. Bobbi Jo had grown up on the Northern Plains, and never expected to meet a Native American blessed with eyes this color.

The message they telegraphed was that she had violated café etiquette.

"I'm sorry, sweetie," the waitress's polite reply held a hint of condescension. "This isn't my table...in fact this whole section is reserved. No one is supposed to sit here. Boss's orders."

"But this is the only empty table in the place. Can't you overlook it just this once?"

"No can do, doll. Rules is rules. I'm sure there'll be a free table soon."

"May I speak to your manager?"

"Not possible. Got himself fired for spending too much time flirting with one of the waitresses. I hear he's pumping gas now. Would you like to speak to the owner, instead?"

"Yes, perhaps that would be better."

"Nah, you don't want to talk to her. Her name's Carley and she's a real bitch. So do us both a favor and move please."

As if on cue, a guy at the cash register tried to get the waitress's attention, "Hey, Carley, can I get my check already? I've gotta get back on the road."

Without turning her attention from Bobbi Jo, she hollered, "Dammit, Donnie, I'll be with you in a second."

"Miss..." Carley tried to maintain her professionalism, "...as you can see, I have neither the time nor the patience for your shenanigans. So please do as I ask and move."

"What a shame. I was just getting comfortable." Bobbi Jo shuffled along the seat. "That's your husband working across the street, isn't it?"

The waitress gave her a wary look. "Yeah, that's Fred... why do you ask?"

"Well, he bragged so much about your service and food,

I couldn't pass it up. Oh well, I guess, I'll just go and see whether he has any candy bars."

Carley checked her watch and tutted, "Fine, if you promise to eat quickly, you can take the table."

Smiling, Bobbi Jo settled back into the booth. "Please may I have a cup of coffee?"

"Do not tell me this whole squabble is over a damn cup of coffee?"

"Not at all, I plan on filling my stomach."

"As long as you do so within the next hour."

"Why? What happens? Does the table turn into a pumpkin?"

"No, but the regulars who use it will make sure your exit is not an enjoyable one."

"We'll see. Now, about that coffee...why don't you throw a couple of eggs and toast in with it."

Without bothering to jot it down, Carley shouted through to the kitchen, "Pete, I need a number one, pronto."

True to Fred's promise, the food and service...once Carley stopped being a bitch...was impeccable.

While she ate, Bobbi Jo noticed how understaffed the place was. Carley and the other poor waitress were bouncing from table to table. The one next to hers had been calling for a refill of their coffee for going on ten minutes.

Clearing her own table, Bobbi Jo walked behind the counter, unnoticed by Carley and dumped her dishes in the appropriate bin. Grabbing an apron from a hook, she tied it around her waist and began checking to see who needed a refill.

Halfway around the café, she bumped into Carley. The waitress was about to reprimand the interfering busybody, when she noticed the tables beyond had been taken care of.

Leaning close, Carley whispered, "Don't think this is gonna get you out of paying your bill, and don't think you're gonna keep any of the tips, either."

Bobbie Jo nodded and was about to continue when Carley hooked her by the arm. "And come talk to me after the shift."

The café stayed busy until nearly closing time. By then, Bobbi Jo had screwed up the courage to promote herself from coffee server to taking orders.

The other waitress, Suzie, gave Bobbi Jo a pad and stood over her shoulder as the latter bungled her way through the first couple of tables.

"Don't worry, sugar, you'll get it," Suzie encouraged. "Hell, I thought Carley would serve me up as the house special my first day. Good thing our people frown on killing one's child."

Suzie's joke prompted Bobbi Jo to study her keenly. Although the younger woman had inherited many of her mother's physical features...including her brilliant blue eyes...her skin tone was much fairer. Bobbi Jo supposed that came from her father.

Bobbi Jo pried, "Does your mom mind you calling her by her first name?"

"Only at work...otherwise she'd be feeding me a bar of Lifebuoy soap. Mind that does taste better than Pete's mystery soup."

109

The pair shared a laugh before going their separate ways to serve the remaining customers.

At six, Fred appeared, and Bobbi Jo observed the dynamics between the three. His appearance earned him a kiss on the cheek from his daughter and one on the lips from his wife.

Fred settled into one of the booths to wait for his family to finish.

His daughter took him a plate of meatloaf and potatoes, immediately making herself comfortable across from him and began picking at the food on his plate, telling him all about what happened in the café today...especially the new girl mom had hired.

Carley stopped next to Bobbi Jo and watched the interaction between her husband and daughter. "We've lost her already. I swear she only cozies up to her dad to get out of work, and he falls for it every time. Come on, you might as well help me clean the kitchen, so we can get out of here."

Following Carley, Bobbi Jo joked, "I don't remember being offered or accepting a job."

"You did the minute Suzie handed you the pad. You made it through the interview by not spilling any coffee on the customers. Though, perhaps I'm being presumptuous. You from around here or just passing through?"

"Like Schrödinger's cat, kinda both.

"Whose cat?"

"Schrödin— never mind, not important. I'm staying at a motor court down the road."

"Oh yeah, I know the place...it's a dump."

"It's not too bad. Bed's comfy and I get a couple of channels on the TV."

"So...yes or no?"

"About?"

"Working? What else could I mean? I'm sure staying out there isn't cheap and I know there's nothing near the motel where you can buy food. One of the perks of working here."

"Fine...with benefits like that, how can I refuse?"

"Great, I expect you here by six tomorrow. We work six to six every day except Sunday. We only catch the church crowd then. Probably won't need you that day."

"And pay?"

"Oh, yeah. Eighty cents an hour plus tips."

Bobbi Jo knew waitstaff got the short end of minimum wage because of *generous* tipping from patrons. Still, having extra money meant not having to spend all of Gladys's cash.

"Deal," she agreed.

"Great, and by the way, what name do I put on your paycheck? I'm sure my darling daughter forgot to ask."

Bobbi Jo thought for a moment. "My name is Josephine—"

"Hold it right there. Don't even think of lying to me, girl. I already raised one daughter through the teenage years, so I know what the truth looks like and what's about to come out of your mouth ain't it. You still want a job here, give me your real name. Whatever you're hiding from, you'll be safe with me."

Bobbi Jo answered softly, "Roberta Josephine Fletcher, though my family used to call me Bobbi Jo."

"Used to?"

"A story I'd rather not get into right now."

"Then Jo it is."

It was after eight by the time Bobbi Jo and Carley finished.

After bidding the family a good night...and swearing on her ancestors that she would show up for her scheduled shift...Bobbi Jo sat in the DeSoto at the café's exit.

A full moon hung low in the crystal clear sky and, acknowledging the sensible move would be to track down Clarence Fulbright in daylight, the urge to, at least, check his residence was too strong to pass up.

Retrieving the paper map from her purse, she turned on the dome light to get directions. Studying it briefly, she got her bearings. Cranking the wheel to the right, she headed into the city.

From time to time, as she drove, she matched the street signs to the map. The route was taking her deeper into the city.

At last, Bobbi Jo located First Street.

She took a left into an old neighborhood, its houses packed tightly together. Whoever built the place had left barely enough room for a driveway between each building.

Slowly cruising down the American Elm-lined road, Bobbi Jo read the house numbers on the mailboxes, eventually coming to 917.

The brakes screeched when she came to a stop in front of the house. Leaning across to the passenger side window, she saw the house was dark and lacked curtains.

She had a sinking feeling as she climbed out of her car.

Stopping at the mailbox, she checked for contents. All she could find were a couple of old sales flyers and the spring *Wards* catalog from 1963 addressed to Daryl Fulbright or occupant.

Making her way along the sidewalk, Bobbi Jo climbed the concrete steps to the porch.

Peering through the glass, she found the interior bare.

As far as she could see, not a stick of furniture graced the house.

Carefully, she crept across the wooden planks to the front door and twisted the doorknob, which was locked.

Bobbi Jo decided to sneak around to the rear, just in case the back door happened to be open. She jumped off the side of the porch, got her foot tangled in the unkept bushes, and stumbled over the downspout.

The neighbors' porch light popped on and their door flew open to reveal an elderly man armed with an equally aged rifle.

For the second time in her life, Bobbi Jo stared down the barrel of a gun.

"Freeze where you are, mister, and put your hands up," the man ordered, yelling over his shoulder, "Gertie, call the police and tell 'em I caught me a cat burglar."

"Oh, for the love of God, Jacob Oliver, put that blunderbuss down before you hurt yourself."

"Dammit, Gertie, don't sass me and do what I tell ya."

Bobbi Jo saw a diminutive woman, with snow white hair, join the man on the porch. Her fingers curled around the barrel forcing it downward.

"Everybody in the state of Oklahoma knows this piece of junk couldn't fire even if you threw it into a furnace."

Squinting into the shadows between the houses, Gertie saw the person her husband was threatening to shoot.

Seeing a female trembling with her hands up, Gertie reprimanded Jacob angrily, "You fool, go get your spectacles. That's a woman ya idjit."

"It's dark out here, how the hell am I supposed to tell? And if she's *not* up to no good then why in the name of Sam Houston is she here this late anyway?"

"He has a point, sweetie, what are you up to?" Gertie's tone gentled to that of a caring grandmother.

"I'm sorry for the ruckus, ma'am," Bobbi Jo replied shakily. "I'm from the State." She was quite proud of her burgeoning talent for inventing identities. "Do you know the gentleman who lives here?"

"Oh, deary, there hasn't been anybody there since those two nice brothers left some time ago. I'm not exactly sure where they went. They just kinda disappeared. Left the house vacant."

Gertie, paused. "Well, except that awful, older man who stayed with them. I don't know if he was related to them or not. The entire neighborhood could hear him yelling at those poor boys all the time."

"Really? Do you remember what he looked like?"

He usually kept to himself...and for good reason. His face..." a shiver ran down Gertie's back as she recalled his appearance, "...he had a terrible scar on his face, looked like he'd been burned, and he wore an eyepatch like a 'B' movie pirate."

Gertie, being the block gossip, had her opinion as to the reason. "I'm guessing he was one of those unfortunate souls who survived the Pearl Harbor attack. I heard a lot of them sailors received dreadful burns from jumping into the oil fires when the ships sank."

Canting her head, Gertie asked suddenly, "Aren't you a little young to be working for the State—"

"Parole Board, ma'am."

"Why on Earth would the state be looking for either of those boys? Though I could understand if it was their roommate."

"Unfortunately, ma'am I'm not at liberty to say."

Faking a sob, Bobbi Jo added a bit of superfluous information to see whether she could wheedle any more information from the woman.

"I just graduated from Oklahoma State, and this is my first assignment. I don't know what I'm supposed to tell my supervisor, tomorrow. I mean my first parolee looks like he skipped, and how is it fair they gave me somebody who's had a couple of months head start?"

"I don't know if it's any help, but when the house was packed up, it was done by local movers.

"Preacher's...Teacher's...something like that."

"For Chrissakes, Gertie, your eyesight is worse than mine. It was Reacher's on Tecumseh."

Patting her husband on the back as if she were rewarding a puppy for miraculously performing its first trick, Gertie exclaimed, "That's it, Jacob. What do you know, you are good for something after all."

Turning back to Bobbi Jo, she suggested, "You might try there first. I'm sure they would have records on where the furniture went."

"I don't know how I can ever thank you two for all your help," Bobbi said appreciatively.

"It is a shame those poor boys fell off the straight and narrow," Gertie lamented. "I hope you can find them quickly. When you do, please remember the church Jacob and I attend has a great outreach program, which I'm sure would be of benefit to them."

"I'll keep that in mind. If you will excuse me, and once again, I apologize for disturbing you, and wish you both a pleasant evening."

Returning to her car, Bobbi Jo wrote the name and address of the movers on the map of the city.

Happy with what she had learned, Bobbi Jo addressed her reflection in the rearview mirror, "Go figure he'd give them a phony address. I bet the state parole board would be interested in finding out...that is if I didn't have plans for him myself."

Starting the engine, she put the DeSoto into gear and drove back to the Hodge Podge Motor Lodge.

Chapter Eleven

Bobbi Jo met Carley in the parking lot. Both had beaten the sunrise.

Carley was happy to note her new hire seemed diligent, and that maybe Suzie *had* inherited her mother's judgment about people.

Not quite ready to admit that to Bobbi Jo, she advised sternly as she unlocked the door, "Don't be making a habit of showing up so early. I don't pay overtime."

"Maybe not, but you did promise meals...and I'm holding you to that."

"I did? I don't remember any such thing—"

"Oh, no you don't. Eggs and bacon, please. Enough for the two of us."

"Yes, boss. Right away." Carley gave a mock salute and, firing up the kitchen, had breakfast ready in no time.

The pair sat at the counter, chatting while they ate.

Carley told Bobbi Jo about the history of the café. How her parents had opened the place after her dad returned from fighting in the Great War.

"Mom passed it on to me after I married Fred. We'd just come back from serving in the army during World War II."

"You were in the army?"

"Why should that surprise you?"

"Well, you don't strike me as somebody who takes orders well."

"Who said I was the one taking orders?"

Bobbi Jo tried to picture what Carley could have possibly done during the war. "So were you a nurse or something?"

"Let's just say...or something.

"Anyway, Mom always said it was a good thing Dad had passed on when Fred and I got hitched because knowing her little girl had married a white man would have killed him."

Bobbi Jo was not sure whether she should laugh or not, so she let it pass.

"Suzie will be next to get the place when her husband—"

"Wait, she's married? Isn't she too young to be? I mean she's what...sixteen?"

Carley chortled. "I wish. No, my precious offspring is twenty. Her husband's not only the son of one of the tribal elders, he's also a medic stationed at Camp Lejeune. He should be out next year."

Little did they know that a run-in between ships of the US and North Vietnamese navies would send Suzie's husband to the jungles of Vietnam for an extended tour.

As much as Carley wanted to know about her new employee's background, the girl remained tight-lipped, more interested in hearing Carley's stories instead.

She caught Bobbi Jo staring over at the booth she had sat in the day before.

"Go ahead and ask your question, girl, before you chew through your lip."

"Is that table really on permanent reserve, or were you just shitting me?"

"No, there's a bunch of roughnecks—"

Bobbi Jo shot Carley a puzzled glance.

"Ya know...roughnecks...the guys who work out in the oilfields. There's a company runs a large field a few miles from here. They operate twenty-four/seven, and the guys work in rotating shifts. They stop in during their lunches and the end of their days for food. They eat well and tip well, so darn tootin' I'll give them preferential treatment. Unless I tell you otherwise, leave that table to me."

"Sure, sure, not a problem." Bobbi Jo nodded absently, but she wasn't thinking about tips. "Are there a lot of well drilling companies in town?"

The two finished the food and Carley collected their plates. "Yeah, there's a bunch of small ones, but Driller's Oil I think is the biggest employer in town.

"Why? Are you suddenly in the market for a husband? Take my word, unless you fancy being greasy the rest of your life, I'd look elsewhere. It just so happens I know a few young bucks who would love to show you a good time."

"I'll pass, *mom*." Bobbi Jo grinned. "Haven't reached the settling down age yet."

"Don't come whining to me when you realize you lost your chance."

"It's funny. A lot of people have been telling me that lately. How about we get to work and finish preparing for the first customers."

"Sounds good. Donnie will be back through first thing, and I hate listening to him bellyache about his coffee not being ready."

True to Carley's word, Donnie was jiggling the café's front door before she could even get it opened. Blocking his entrance, she handed him a large thermos of coffee and, as an added treat, a paper bag containing a bear claw he had not even thought of ordering.

"Now, you ungrateful cur, get your butt in gear so you're back in time for lunch. I'll settle ya up then."

"You know, Carley, one day I'm gonna find a better place, minus insults," Donnie threatened.

"Donald Martin, you know damn well you'll never find any better food. Especially one run by the people who treat you like family," Carley scolded.

Like a docile puppy, Donnie mumbled, "Yes, ma'am. I'll see ya at noon," and trudged to his eighteen-wheeler.

Bobbi Jo watched in amazement at the way Carley handled the gruff trucker.

"Aren't you afraid of losing a customer...let alone the money for the food you just gave him...if he actually finds a new café?"

"Hardly. He knows I will track him down and take what little hair is left on his scalp."

Carley's chortle of laughter left Bobbi Jo wondering whether she was serious.

The morning was busier than the previous day. In addition to the truckers and tourists, Bobbi Jo got her first glimpse of the men from the oilfield. As they made their way to their usual table, Carley greeted them with the same flippant warmth, she had Donnie.

"Well, it's about damn time you lazy oafs finally showed up. I had Pete make an extra-large pot of oatmeal for the lot of ya, and none of ya had the decency to stop."

"Thank God the boss decided to treat us to a surprise celebratory barbeque," the eldest roughneck replied with a grin. "I'm not sure my colon could have handled any of Pete's wallpaper paste."

The table broke out in a riotous guffaw.

"Just for that, Mac, I'll have him dig it out of the garbage can and give you a double helping."

Mac had a better idea, "Rather you bring us the *House Special* without the oatmeal."

"Really now?" Carley arched an eyebrow. "Some rich aunt kick the bucket and leave you her fortune?"

"More or less," Mac reassured her, pulling a wad of cash from his dirty shirt pocket. "Bonuses came in. So go fire up the stove...we're starving."

Carley snatched the money before he changed his mind. Thumbing through the roll, she ribbed, "You're getting old, Mac. Didn't used to be this easy to rob ya."

Extending his hand, he said, "Was a long night. Bet you wouldn't try it when I'm wide awake."

She returned the bundle. "By the time you and the boys are done, you'll be sound asleep at the table snoring...no doubt scaring the rest of my customers away. Make sure to leave a generous tip for my trouble.

"Oh, and Fred said he wasn't going to drive you home any more. His car was a greasy mess the last time. I heard about it for days."

"If your hubby doesn't appreciate oil, he's in the wrong business *and* the wrong state."

"Miss Carley," one of the others at the table interjected, "can ya stop flirting with the old man and feed us...please?"

"Only cuz you asked nicely, Rollie. The rest of you could learn a lesson from him."

"Ya mean like how to kiss ass?" one of the others piped up.

Carley rolled her eyes and abandoned Rollie to fend for himself.

Heading to the kitchen with the order, Carley snagged Bobbie Jo's arm and tugged her along.

"I'm assuming you can cook as well as you serve coffee."

"Uh, yeah. At least, my cooking hasn't killed anybody yet."

"Good cuz you were just promoted to assistant chef. Get in there and help Pete. If these boys are loaded I'm sure the rest aren't far behind."

While Pete tended to the rib eyes and hash-browns, Bobbi Jo fried eggs and bacon, making sure the eggs were over-medium, with the yolks just firm enough to ooze when they were cut into.

Carley stood over her new assistant cook's shoulder long enough to be satisfied with her skills.

The pair produced a banquet for the men. The intoxicating aroma in the kitchen wafted out into the dining area, announcing breakfast was on the way.

Pete served up the food, and smacked the bell, signaling the orders were ready.

As Carley appeared to retrieve them, she demoted Bobbi Jo to server. "Grab the other one, doll."

The women resembled a pair of Himalayan Sherpas as they carried the laden trays, which they placed on the table adjacent to the roughnecks, then put a loaded plate in front of each man.

This gave Bobbi Jo a chance to get a better look at them. None were Clarence, at least from what she recalled of him. She was a small child, he was pointing a gun at her. Committing his features to memory was not a priority.

Putting that fact aside, she noticed, while all were freshly showered, traces of dirt and oil clung to their faces as though it had become a permanent part of their complexions.

She could see the night and the strenuous nature of their jobs had wearied them. Their eyes were bleary and bloodshot, but none of that dampened their appetite, or their banter.

Bobbi Jo caught Rollie checking her out. Briefly, their eyes locked. He gave her a wink and smile, to which she responded with the faintest of blushes.

That was all the two had time for, any chance of conversation curtailed by the arrival of the second crew, propelling Bobbi Jo back to the kitchen.

Taking an unscheduled break, she poked her head through the swinging doors. To her dismay, she saw Rollie had left without giving her an opportunity to introduce herself. Frowning, she trudged back to the griddle.

At noon, Carley wandered into the kitchen to fetch Donnie's standing lunch order. While she was dishing up the trucker's Salisbury steak, she spelled Bobbi Jo off griddle duty, telling her to grab some food before returning to the floor.

After slapping a ham and cheese sandwich together, Bobbi Jo slipped out of the café's back door to the payphone along its side. Dropping in a dime, she dialed the phone number she had obtained for the *Reacher Moving and Storage Company*.

After a couple of rings, a woman answered cheerfully, "Reacher Moving. Have truck will travel. This is Wanda."

In a very official sounding voice, Bobbi Jo introduced herself, "Wanda, this is Miss Doris Speckman from the Oklahoma Department of Corrections. It has come to our attention that your company recently moved one of our parolees from 917 First Street without proper authorization. I'm calling to inform you, your company could be charged with aiding and abetting a known felon—"

"Whoa, whoa, whoa, Miss Speckman was it?" Wanda's attitude did an about face. "I can assure you we would never knowingly violate any laws. When exactly did we supposedly do this anyway?"

"Don't get snippy with me, miss. Not unless you want the full weight of the state of Oklahoma to come down on your company."

"Ma'am, I'm only trying to find out the date so I can look it up in our records."

"According to witnesses, it was approximately five or six months ago. I need to know where you moved him to."

"Are you joking? Do you know how many moves we do in a month?"

"Then I suggest you start looking. I will call you tomorrow at this time for the information."

Hanging up the phone with an air of authority, she turned around to see Carley standing behind her, arms crossed.

Carley's expression told Bobbi Jo, she had been privy to the majority of her performance.

In an attempt to deflect the question she could see her employer burning to ask, Bobbi Jo teased, "Jesus, what are you doing sneaking up on me like that? Do you *want* to give me a heart attack?"

"Well, you know what the white men say about the Cherokee...you only hear us coming if we want you to."

The reply left Bobbi Jo speechless. Her brain shifted into *Legitimate Excuse* mode, but nothing cogent could be cobbled together fast enough.

Carley broke the silence. "Let me guess, another story you can't share yet?"

"I can expla—" Bobbi Jo started.

Carley tossed up her hand up, "Not until you can give me the truthful answer, girl. Just get back to work. Suzie is whining that she's starving and accusing me of running a sweatshop."

As Carley turned to head inside, she stopped. Holding a fiver over her shoulder, she said without looking back, "Rollie wanted me to give you this, though, I thought about keeping it myself."

Slowly, Bobbi Jo stepped up behind her and accepted the bill.

"Whatever you're up to, girl, don't hurt the boy. He's a good kid."

Staring down at the bill, Bobbi Jo saw scribbled across it:

Maybe I can serve you dinner next time? along with a phone number.

Transfixed by the message, she contemplated the gesture. Although this was the first time anyone had made what appeared to be a sincere offer, Bobbi Jo's jaded outlook, convinced her he was looking for more than an evening out.

The afternoon breeze seemed to whisper in her ear, "Pay no heed to what she said. If he can be of any use to us, take advantage."

"But how is that fair to—" she whispered back.

"And how was having our lives snatched so indiscriminately fair to us?"

"You're right, Mother. It wasn't."

"Then do not pass up this opportunity."

Bobbi Jo nodded and pocketed the bill before going in. Grabbing a pad, she said to Suzie, "Your mother wants you to go to lunch."

Canting her head, uncertain why Jo sounded sad, Suzie glanced at her mom over Jo's shoulder.

Carley, apparently glaring at the back of Bobbi Jo, jerked her thumb at Suzie toward the kitchen.

And the remainder of the day continued in the same fashion. Carley said nothing to Bobbi Jo, busying herself with the most menial task in order to prevent any chance of conversation.

At closing time she said to Bobbi Jo, "Why don't you leave the cleanup to Suzi and me. I'm sure you have other things you need to tend to."

Even as Bobbi Jo tried to reassure Carley she could help out, Carley handed her a sack lunch and shooed her out of the café.

On the way back to her cabin, she contemplated whether she had been fired.

Pulling into the drive, Bobbi Jo let those thoughts fall by the wayside. The delectable aromas from the bag were tormenting her mushrooming appetite.

"There's nothing I can do either way until tomorrow," she muttered out loud.

If, indeed, this was her last day at the café, the meal now constituted part of her severance package.

Chapter Twelve

The DeSoto chugged down Sixty-six toward the café.

In the predawn darkness, Bobbi Jo's eyes met those staring back at her in the rearview mirror. Bathed in the illumination from the dashboard, her reflection was shrouded by an eerie iridescence.

While acknowledging she was talking to herself, a part of her believed she was actually face to face with her mother. Bobbi Jo was so convinced, she refused to look over her shoulder to prove she had not picked up a spectral hitchhiker.

To take her mind off the eyes staring her down, Bobbi Jo allowed her thoughts to vacillate between resigning before Carley could fire her and begging for her understanding and coming clean about everything.

Neither option excited her, especially the second. It would mean having to admit contributing to Roy's death and coming to Oklahoma City solely to rid the world of Clarence.

With a sigh, she said to the image, "No matter how

many times I run that particular conversation through my head, the only way I can see it ending is with Carley ordering Suzie to call the cops while she holds me at knife-point to make sure I don't run."

Bobbi Jo laughed, humorlessly. "No, since it's Carley, she'd probably pin me to the floor and hold the knife at my throat."

Deciding it was better to change topics altogether, her mind wandered to Rollie whom she had considered calling last night, thankful she didn't have the nerve.

"Could you just imagine that conversation? 'Hi, this is the desperate woman willing to call a stranger who wrote his number on a five dollar bill.' As bad as it sounds in my head, to articulate it is a thousand times worse.

"I don't know about him, but I would have dropped the receiver and disconnected my phone, then probably moved."

In the midst of her humor, a voice reminded, "Never mind the fact you would have to explain the charred tire iron on the floorboard of your car."

Bobbi Jo's and the image's attention darted to the metal bar in front of the passenger seat. It appeared to glow back to life in the greenish light under the dash.

With a smug chuckle, the mirror observed, "I bet any suspicious trooper who might pull you over would see Roy's fingerprints clearly scorched into the metal...minus his missing ring finger of course."

"Shuddup. Just. Shut. Up. There's no way that's true."

"Hmm...maybe, but with the advances in forensics, can you be sure? If I were you, I'd just toss it to the side of the road. Nobody will find it out here."

Bobbi Jo's gaze swung from the tire iron to the eyes in the mirror.

"You're right. Better safe than sorry," she agreed, adding a nod. Of course, her reflection nodded back, reinforcing her decision.

Searching the darkness for any oncoming traffic, all she could see was the broken line rolling into view at the edge of her hi-beams.

Inching over, Bobbi Jo attempted to snag the iron, but it lay just beyond her grasp. Peering at the blacktop once more, she was satisfied she was alone on the road.

Focusing on the tire iron, she lunged, but as her fingers tightened around it, the interior of the car lit up like a prison break...complete with blaring horns.

Straightening up, she realized the DeSoto had drifted across the lane and into the path of a truck. Sharply, she cranked the steering wheel to the right, but over-corrected, sending the vehicle careening back and forth between the lanes. Fortunately, she avoided the truck as it rushed past.

Brakes squealing and with the acrid odor of burning rubber filling her nostrils, Bobbi Jo brought the car to a halt before she ended up in the shallow ditch at the edge of the road.

Panting, and on the verge of tears, she put the car in neutral and engaged the parking brake. Closing her eyes, she rested her head on the steering wheel, until her heart stopped racing.

Finally, still trembling, Bobbi Jo unlatched the handle and let the door swing open.

She found the tire iron wedged in the dip at the back of the seat. Yanking it free, she climbed out of the vehicle and, summoning up a burst of strength, hurled the offending article into the darkness.

Hearing a thunk as it landed somewhere out of sight,

she sank onto her seat, and banged the door shut, reprimanding herself for carelessness.

Surrounded by the welcome silence of an empty road, she continued onto the outskirts of Oklahoma City.

As Bobbi Jo approached the diner, she cursed the morning for showing no mercy. Not only was Carley's car in the lot, but also there were two others.

One she recognized as Pete's old Studebaker, but had no idea who owned the Pontiac.

To make matters worse, although the dining room lights were off, the ones in the kitchen burned brightly.

Quietly, Bobbi Jo rounded the café to the kitchen's entrance. Half expecting it to be bolted shut, relief swept through her to find it open.

Opening the door, Bobbi Jo came face to face with Carley.

"Lose your way?" Carley sniped.

"You wouldn't believe what happened on the way to work."

"Yeah, you're right. I wouldn't. Just make sure it doesn't happen again."

Meekly, Bobbi Jo replied, "Yes, ma'am." and went to grab an apron and pad.

Carley stopped her. "Kitchen duty today, Jo. For some reason the guys liked your food. So, it's you and Pete on the grills."

"Aren't you going to need me on the floor?" Bobbi Jo asked.

"Not today. Fred's niece, Eddie, has come in to help."

That explained the Pontiac.

"She's back from college in California. Have to say those professors have done a good job of screwing her head up. The girl has been spending the whole summer apologizing for everything the white man has ever done to my people.

"Hell, she actually begged me to let her work for free today in some kind of beatnik reparations," Carley said, catching herself flashing a grin at Bobbi Jo for the first time since the phone call. "Can you imagine something so ridiculous?"

Bobbi Jo shook her head.

Carley said, "Get your butt in gear and help Pete open the kitchen."

After peeling and chopping mountains of potatoes and onions for Pete, Bobbi Jo heard the dining section open, and people began to file in. Before long, orders flooded the kitchen.

The whole time the waitresses appeared at the window, shouting their orders, Pete said nothing. He didn't bother reading the order slips, simply memorized everything as they came in.

If he needed Bobbi Jo's help, he flicked a spatula or knife, assuming she would understand his gesture. She had yet to decide whether Pete was simply rude, or a selective mute.

There were a few tense moments when he all but dragged Bobbi Jo by the hand, to point out the stacks of necessary supplies, until she figured it out.

It seemed that useless conversation disrupted his thought process and caused him to confuse orders. Her dad had told her about this syndrome, but she could not remember what it was called. So, she just followed his lead.

The pair ended up humming along like a well-oiled machine.

Whenever she got a chance, Bobbi Jo wandered over to the hatch. She saw her replacement buzzing around the floor, Eddie's deeply-tanned legs, set off nicely by her white go-go boots and short skirt, the source of many a man's admiration.

She looked over to the corner where the roughnecks ate, hoping to spot Rollie among them, but he was nowhere to be seen.

It left her with mixed feelings. She was disappointed he was not there to talk to, then again, he was not around to ogle at a college educated beach bunny like his co-workers.

Returning to the grill, she worked nonstop for the rest of the morning until she felt a hand tap her on the shoulder, and heard Carley's voice in her ear. "I believe you need to make a phone call."

Bobbi Jo stepped away from the grill to let her employer take over.

To avoid any surprises, Bobbi Jo darted through traffic and crossed over to the service station. She saw Fred giving her a curious look as she passed the big window, and replied with a cheery wave.

I'm guessing Carley already told him about the phone

call. No sense rehashing it with him or explaining why I risked life and limb to use his phone booth.

Stepping into the booth, she shut the door to reduce the street noise.

The dime brought the phone to life with a happy chime. Bobbi Jo dialed the main office of Reacher Moving.

It had occurred to her that Wanda might contact the Oklahoma Department of Corrections to verify the caller's legitimacy or to confirm she had the necessary documentation — to Bobbi Jo's detriment.

"Reacher Moving. Have truck will travel," Wanda answered the phone blandly.

"Good afternoon, Wanda, this is—"

"I know full well who this is. I've been waiting all morning for your call."

Bobbi Jo bit her lip to curb her mirth at the woman's abrupt change of manner. "Oh really? Why is that?"

"Because you caused me to be here until almost half past two this morning looking for the documents you requested."

"And did you find them?"

"I did and I also spoke with our company's lawyer."

"You did, eh? And what did he tell you?"

"We cannot be held responsible for moving a third party. We would have no reason to know he was on parole."

"But I'm betting he suggested you assist us in finding him. Kind of a good will gesture."

The line went quiet for a moment. "Yes...and please ensure your superiors are aware of that."

"And where did your company spirit our boy off to?"

"There were actually two trucks requested by that address. The first was requested for April eighth..."

"And where did it end up?"

"The other side of the city. 6514 Comanche Trail. You know the houses owned by the oil company on the east side of the city...Drillers."

"Okay, thank..."

The import of Wanda's previous statement, registered.

"Wait...did you say there was a second move?" This was a tidbit Gertie had forgotten to share.

"Yeah, on the twenty-second. He was a real treat according to the driver."

For some reason, Bobbi Jo felt it important to ask, "Did the move require a large truck?"

"No, according to the invoice, he used one of our smaller ones. The invoice lists a couple of trunks and some bedroom furniture. Not much for what it cost him."

"Where did the stuff end up?"

"Truckee, California."

"What's the address?"

The line went quiet again, except for the sound of papers being flipped.

"Hmm...that's strange."

"What is?"

"There's no house address. Just a storage warehouse. Butterman's on Donner Pass Road."

"Okay, thank you for your help."

"Don't you want to know what we moved in the first—"

Once again, Bobbi Jo hung up on the woman.

"Caught you, Buchanan," she crowed.

Exiting the booth, she walked to the curb opposite the café, to see someone on the other side waving at her.

Squinting, she recognized Rollie Johnston.

Looking both ways, she hurried across the street to meet him, delighted by the pleasant surprise his presence engendered, and fought the urge to hug him just for being there.

Instead, she asked with a concerned tone, "Why are you so late? Did something happen in the field?"

"No, and I want to apologize for missing breakfast."

The clothes he was wearing appeared to have been freshly bought and only slightly ironed.

Watching him squirm uncomfortably in them, like a kid about to get his school pictures, made Bobbi Jo smile.

"Hey, no stress. I'm sure you were busy. What brings you by then?"

"Ummm....since you didn't call me last night, I was wondering if you'd be interested in going out with me tonight?"

Before Bobbi Jo's brain caught up with her mouth, she heard herself reply, "That would be cool."

"You okay if I choose?"

"Sure. I'm still new around here and don't know many places."

"Great, I'll pick you up here after work."

"Hang on, what about my car?"

"I'm sure Carley won't mind you leaving it here."

Knowing Carley, Bobbi Jo thought cynically, *she will probably slit my tires.*

"Sure, Rollie, that sounds like a plan."

To say Bobbi Jo was anything but thrilled with Rollie's choice of venues was putting it mildly. While she did not expect French food and bottles of expensive wine, to be sitting in a bowling alley munching on French fries and swilling beer was not what she classified as a dinner date.

Irritating her more was the fact she was stuck watching Rollie and the boys league bowl.

Grumpily, she shoved a handful of fries in her mouth. "I can't believe I put on makeup for this."

The only chance Bobbi Jo got to talk to Rollie was between frames when he came over to the table to steal some fries. No sooner had he sat down and started a conversation, than they called him back to bowl.

Between games, the boys took a break to restock their beer supply. Rollie joined Bobbi Jo with another bottle for her.

"I'm really sorry about this," he said remorsefully, seeing the disappointed look on her face. "When you didn't call me last night, I wanted to hurry up this morning and ask ya out before anybody else had the chance. Heard there was a line forming."

Taking a sip of her beer, Bobbi Jo shrugged slightly, not saying anything.

"I promise to make it up to you," Rollie all but pleaded.

"Just make sure it's not on league night next time," Bobbi Jo granted him a smile from behind the bottle.

"I promise, doll," Rollie promised happily. "Wouldn't have tonight, but I totally forgot about the company tourney when I asked."

"Hey, Rollie," a voice from the lanes called. "Stop flirting with your girl and get back down here. You're up."

Bobbi Jo shot daggers at the guy, not sure whether it was because he interrupted their first real conversation since they arrived...or being referred to as Rollie's girl.

A little presumptuous, you jerk.

Rollie excused himself, leaving Bobbi Jo to study the place from her chair.

With its twenty-five lanes, it was the largest bowling alley she had ever been in but, as with every bar and pool hall, it shared the same stale stench of cigarettes and beer.

A new aroma permeated this venue. The scent of deodorant being sprayed into sweaty shoes.

Bored with watching Rollie's team getting beaten, Bobbie Jo got up to stretch her legs.

Walking down the dining area behind the lanes, Bobbi Jo greeted the guys she recognized from the café.

She was surprised to see Mac was not bowling on the same team as Rollie. Seeing his scores were in the 280's, she figured it would have been a waste of his skills.

He was loitering by the rack of balls waiting his turn, and she snuck up behind him to jab him in the ribs, giggling when he flinched.

"I see you're a traitor to your crew," Bobbi Jo accused.

"Bah," he said with a wink. "I carry their deadwood enough in the field."

"That's pretty harsh."

"But true."

Mac watched as the guy bowling ahead of him picked up an incredible seven-ten split, prompting both teams to cheer.

"Well, my fair maiden, if you excuse me, I need to leave a better impression on those sad sacks."

"Knock 'em dead, Mac."

By the time she reached the end of the lanes, the scent of cigarette smoke stirred a need for one. Locating the cigarette machine, she waited, almost patiently, for an older man to retrieve his pack from the slot.

Patting her pockets, Bobbi Jo discovered they were empty.

The man straightened up, his back to her.

Bobbi Jo studied him as she considered bumming one off of him...less than politely.

He was considerably taller than she. His head bald except a ring of white hair circling the back.

He was dressed in a bowling shirt with the picture of a bowling ball electrocuting a bunch of pins. The shirt proclaimed him as a proud member of the *Lightning Strikes*.

How tacky. You should see what a lightning strike does to something, Bobbi thought as she decided to tap him on the back.

Glancing over his shoulder, he saw the girl looking at him. "Yeah? Whatcha need?" he asked gruffly.

"Um, I was hoping you might see it in your heart to spare a smoke..."

Chuckling, he tapped one up. Offering her a light, he smirked. "Ya know, you skirts are all the same..."

Bobbi Jo did not hear anything else he said. Her brain froze on the way he said *skirts*. The lit cigarette almost falling from her mouth.

She had heard it used with the same disdain only once before. That dreadful day when he and his brother were trying to break their way through her bedroom door.

The words echoed loudly in her ears as he yelled at her mom, "Open up the goddamn door, ya fucking skirt, or so help me, I'm gonna take great pleasure in making ya suffer when I get in there."

Narrowing her eyes, she recognized him. Even if prison had aged him, this was Clarence Fulbright.

Had Bobbi Jo possessed so much as a rusty spoon, she

would have plunged it into the man's chest. Right through where his name was stitched, egotistically, into his shirt.

"What's with you?" he asked, unsure of the girl's suddenly brooding stink eye. "Din't your mother ever teach you to be grateful and say *thank you*? Damn kids nowadays."

Tired of trying to figure out the lack of manners of today's youth, he pushed by her and back to his game.

Bobbi Jo kept an eye on the lane where Clarence and his team were bowling.

Her hard focus brought Rollie to her table, concerned she had met someone else while his attention was otherwise engaged.

"You okay?"

"Oh, uh, yeah. Are you about done?"

"Just finished. You must be my good luck charm. Bowled my best series ever."

Bobbi Jo nodded abstractedly, not really listening. She watched as Clarence and another guy packed their stuff up and went out to the lot.

She asked Rollie, "We ready to go then?"

"Sure, you still hungry? I know I could use a burger."

For a moment, Bobbi Jo considered asking Rollie where he lived, assuming he had a place in company housing as well, but thought better of it.

She knew how this game was played, not naive enough to believe, even with a guy as nice as Rollie, he would misconstrue the meaning of her question. It did not even make sense to her when she ran it back through her head.

Reason advised, *You managed to keep your virginity in a brothel...don't be stupid and* accidentally *give it away tonight.*

"Nah, I'm tired and have to work early tomorrow. How about just dropping me off at my car."

Mustering up a smile, she offered, "I promise to cook you up something nice if you stop by for breakfast in the morning."

Relief swept through Rollie, thinking he had managed to salvage a second date. "You have a deal."

As they drove back to the café, the surrounding area was closed up for the night.

The only streetlight illuminated was the one in the back of the café where Bobbi Jo had parked. She leaned over to give Rollie a quick peck on the cheek, scooting out of the car before he could get friendly.

Climbing into the DeSoto, she fired it up and sat there for a moment, acting like she was adjusting her seat.

Bobbi Jo waited until Rollie waved and drove away.

Giving him a five minute head start, she put the car in gear and set off to Comanche Trail.

Chapter Thirteen

B obbi Jo switched off her headlights a few houses up
the block from 6514 Comanche Trail. She parked
across the street from the ranch-style duplex, the
two residences connected by their garages.

The windows for 6512 were burning brightly even at
this late hour. Bobbi Jo watched the tenants buzz about the
house.

In contrast, 6514 was dark and brooding. Unlike its
neighbors, the grass was in desperate need of a manicure. If
Bobbi Jo had not been informed of the contrary, the place
had the air of abandonment, which gave her an uneasy
feeling.

She maintained her vigilance for the next hour, trying
to bolster her nerves by comparing herself with the radio
detectives she listened to as a kid, while chastising herself
for neglecting to bring a thermos of coffee.

That's what good cops do.

She glanced up and down the dimly lit street, there
were no vehicles approaching. She checked her watch, it
was past midnight.

Bobbi Jo cursed Fulbright under her breath. "Damn you, Clarence, where the hell are you?"

She was torn between returning to the cabin so she didn't miss work in the morning, and making the trip worthwhile.

Getting out of the car, she closed the door quietly and, padding across the street, snuck around the back of the house, taking care not to trip over anything this time.

At the back door, she cupped her hands around the sides of her eyes and peered into the dark kitchen. As far as she could make out, the place was fully furnished...somebody lived here.

Trying to get a better view, she thought she saw a dark shape dart across the kitchen floor. She was concentrating on the spot when the angry face of a Doberman pinscher pounced up to the door, snarling and barking.

Bobbi Jo got such a shock, she jerked backwards and tumbled off the step, flailing wildly.

Picking herself off the dirt, she dashed to her car. Inside the house, the Doberman was still barking.

Bobbi Jo feared the block would light up at the noise, but the houses remained quiet. With the exception of 6512, from where she heard someone yell, "Goddammit, Fritz, shut the hell up."

The dog's full weight thudded against the front door and she thanked God the locks held.

Looking forward to curling up in a warm bed, she climbed into the DeSoto and drove away without a backward glance, keeping the lights off until she cleared the block.

This would not be the last time she paid a visit to 6514 Comanche Trail.

Images of Clarence's face made it impossible for Bobbi Jo to get a decent night's sleep. Eventually she gave up and, long before her alarm went off she was showered and on her way to the diner.

To her surprise, Bobbi Jo beat Carley to the café, though it meant she was compelled to endure the morning chill of an early fall.

Twenty minutes later, her engine running to keep warm and her gas dwindling, she spotted the flash of a stacked set of headlights on high beam, reflected in her rearview mirror.

The accompanying loud rumble, the unmistakeable sound of a hole in a muffler, indicated it was Carley's marlin blue and whitecap white 1960 International B100 Travelall wagon arriving. Seeing her employer behind the wheel of the behemoth, never failed to amuse her.

Carley was gathering her stuff off the passenger seat when Bobbi Jo knocked on her window. Rolling down the glass, Carley said, "Don't say it. I already know Wesa needs her muffler fixing."

"Ya know, the only comparison between your wagon and a cat is that they are both temperamental and growl like they're about to attack. Ya should call her Kanuna—"

"Bullfrog? Why is that Miss White Woman?"

"They both make too much noise."

They shared a laugh. The first in a couple of days.

"Why haven't you got your beast fixed yet? Your husband runs a service station doesn't he?"

"Yep, which means I'm the last one to be scheduled and the first to be bumped if the daft nugget overbooks his schedule. Oh, and remind me to stop Suzie teaching you Cherokee on your breaks. Don't need you to understand what I'm saying about you behind your back."

"Too late...she already taught me those words," Bobbi Jo arched a brow at Carley. "She inherited her mother's stubbornness. Do you think either of us could stop her?"

Carley alighted, raising her eyebrows at Bobbi Jo's puffy eyes and dark circles.

"Enjoyable night with Rollie?"

"Only if you enjoy watching men throw their balls at pins, and how did you know?"

"Who do you think sent him to wait for you to come back from Fred's? In the future, just use the phone over here. I had to dock you five minutes for being late returning from lunch."

"I think you need to check your watch, ma'am, I reckon it's running fast."

"My payroll...my time. Oh, and fix your makeup. Don't need my customers worrying that a rabid raccoon got loose in the café."

Bobbi Jo flipped the bird at Carley's back as they walked to the kitchen entrance.

Carley chuckled. "I saw that."

The week continued as usual. Donnie turned up promptly at six for his coffee and daily dose of Carley hospitality. The guys came in from the fields for breakfast, lunch, and dinner.

The only difference was Rollie.

He turned up immediately after his shift for one of

Bobbi Jo's specially cooked breakfasts. Carley claimed the tips Rollie left, reasoning she was entitled to them for having to suffer the flirting between cook and customer.

In truth, what others saw as flirting was Bobbi Jo's way of getting information about the oil fields and the other employees Rollie might know.

He told her about oil gushers, and the hardships and headaches of his job. Likewise, as if the oil field was little more than a close knit small town, he gossiped like an old lady regarding who was doing what with whose wife.

It made Bobby Jo laugh to listen.

Not once, did he mention Clarence Fulbright.

Bobbi Jo presumed he kept to himself or only hung out with those on his bowling team.

After work, she drove to his house in an attempt to figure out his routine. Each night, she studied the structure of the residence.

By the fourth night, she was trying to determine whether it was possible to entice the dog out.

Drugging a piece of meat maybe?

Then what?

Set the house on fire?

Deep in thought, Bobbi Jo neglected to notice the head-lights rolling up behind her. It wasn't until her passenger side door opened, triggering the dome light, that she jumped into action.

"Hold your horses, Pocahontas," a female ordered. "Unless you want me to kick your butt?"

Making herself comfortable on the bench seat of the DeSoto, Carley eased the door shut.

"What the hell are you doing loitering outside a house that's not Rollie's? And don't bother lying. I want the truth for once," Carley ordered in her mom-voice. "All of it."

Bobbi Jo glanced at the dark house and then, like a geyser bursting out of the ground, let the whole story flow.

She told Carley about the day at Donner Pass, her family's murder, bouncing around the Midwest as a kid, and what she had done in Milwaukee, concluding with her time in St Louis.

Taking a breath, not bothering to control her emotions or tears, she went on.

"I-I killed Roy there," she said with a shaky voice. "But he got what he deserved!"

"Wait? You did *what*?" Carley asked, not believing her ears. "How did you kill him?"

Bobbi Jo confessed her crime in great detail. As her dad had told her, catharsis was good for the soul...and she could repress it no longer.

"I tried to crush his skull in with a tire iron."

Carley canted her head and repeated, *"Tried?"*

Bobbi Jo nodded going onto describe how he had blocked the attack and ended up with the iron. "He was about to batter me with it when he got struck by lightning. Next best thing to the electric chair," Bobbi Jo said with the ghost of a grin.

"But you didn't kill him. Most they could get you for is battery." The irony of the charge was not wasted on Carley. Not wanting to laugh outright, she added, "Or maybe failure to report a death..."

"I-I don't believe you. I watched him die in front of me."

"By an act of God or a demonstration of electrical conductivity. Which brings us to why you are sitting in front of this house. I guess the *why* isn't so much the issue. It's more like the *how*? How were you planning to carry this off?" Carley pried.

Bobbi Jo's gaze slid back to the house.

"Burning it down won't work unless you want to kill the family next door, too. And no, I won't let you do that. Besides, the fire department and ambulances would be here before he even got to be medium rare."

"Then, genius, do you have a better plan?"

"Maybe. Whatever it is, starts with you giving up your nightly stalking. You're way too conspicuous."

"Huh? You realize what you volunteered to do?"

"I do. In my culture family means everything, so I understand your need for justice. While I can't wholeheartedly condone the taking of a life, neither can I stand by and watch you screw this up and end up either in jail or dead...if the tale of your last attempt is any example of your skill.

"Now, let's go back to the café. I need coffee."

As Carley put her hand on the door, Bobbi Jo asked, "By the way, how did I not hear Kanuna?"

"I told you to call her Wesa. My husband does run a service station, remember?"

"But you kept telling me you were the last on the list."

"Well, I lodged a complaint with the owner and she had a conversation with Fred."

"The owner?" Bobbi Jo quizzed.

"Yes, who just happens to be my mom. He's more afraid of her than he is of me. She can be a real bitch at times. She may not run either business directly, but she still owns the choicest real estate on Route Sixty-six."

"I thought she gave everything to you?"

"No, just the headaches and, speaking of which, I could have saved you a world of pain if you had confided in me in the first place, girl. Mac is not only a crew chief, but the shift manager for all the night crews. I could have gotten any information from him just by asking.

"Oh well, too late to worry about that now. Follow me back to the café. I'm sure you haven't eaten yet."

Over coffee and pastries, the two hatched their plan, which was refined during the subsequent week.

It started with Carly posting notices in the café that they would be closed the coming Monday so she could attend to tribal business.

Fred never questioned his wife's decisions to take a day off because it was so rare an occurrence.

Her promise that he did not have to accompany her to the Cherokee Nation, made him agree with even more enthusiasm. He had never seen eye to eye with his mother-in-law when it came to the operation of the businesses, and always ended up in heated disagreements, which spoiled any attempt to remain civil.

As for Bobbi Jo, Carley had her familiarize herself with the road to the oil fields, instructing her to stop at the foot of the hill approximately five miles from the highway...far enough from the gates to avoid detection by security.

By the time the day rolled around, she was sure she could drive the road with her eyes closed.

The next part of the plan was simple and one Bobbi Jo was more than happy to do.

It required her to spend Saturday night scrubbing her room from top to bottom. With the help of a strong liquid detergent, Bobbi Jo removed every trace of her existence from the cabin.

Once completed, she did as Carley had advised and

slept on top of the quilts, wearing a pair of cotton gloves to make sure she did not touch anything.

On Sunday, Bobbi Jo checked the room twice to verify she had not left any personal belongings.

Leaving the cabin cleaner than when she arrived, Bobbi Jo stopped at the office to settle her bill.

The woman behind the counter feigned a frown that her only guest was leaving. "It's a shame you're not staying longer," she lamented. "You were so quiet, I almost forgot you were here."

"Except when rent was due," Bobbi Jo retorted.

The woman chose to ignore the slight. "Is there a forwarding address?" she asked instead.

"Just the Milwaukee one I checked in with. I've decided to head back."

"I'm happy to hear that."

Taking the payment for the last couple of days, the woman wished her well and hoped she would return in the future.

Bobbi Jo left without bidding the clerk farewell. It was something Carley had suggested so her departure would be remembered.

Climbing into the DeSoto, Bobbi Jo turned the car to the east, glad when the Hodge Podge Motor Lodge disappeared from sight.

Abiding by Carley's directions, Bobbi Jo took the back roads into the city, speculating in earnest, as she drove, about her employer. Throughout the entire scheme, Carley had remained calm and methodical.

It made Bobbi Jo wonder whether she had killed people during the war and, if so, how often?

She reached the outskirts of Oklahoma City around noon. As instructed, she parked her car in the service bay at the gas station, which Carley had left unlocked, and closed it behind her.

She spent the rest of Sunday and a sleepless Sunday night there.

Early the next morning, she saw the gleam of headlights through the high windows of the garage door. Cautiously, she peeked out to see Carley's Travelall pull up.

Watching a figure alight from the truck, she caught the tail-end of a conversation, which, she surmised, had been going on for several minutes.

Fred was in the middle of a sentence, when the passenger side door clanged shut, and two silhouettes faced each other.

"...but won't your Ma get upset about losing income from *both* the café and service station being closed today? And why am I dropping you off here, at this godforsaken hour?"

Hands on her hips, Carley's exasperated tone suggested she had reached the end of the topic...and possibly her tether.

"Fred, I already told you, Mom wants to meet Suzie's first hire. Jo is up for it. It's a three hour drive, so an early start gives us longer at the reservation. Did I miss anything?"

"Why aren't you driving?"

"Because like this conversation...I'm tired and if I can use her gas all the better. But if you'd rather come instead—"

"Oh, God no." Fred shuddered.

"Then shut up and stop asking questions. Go home and enjoy your day off before I change my mind and make you scrub the café's kitchen."

Bobbi Jo did not hear Fred's reply, but smiled when she saw him embrace his wife, Carley rising to her tiptoes to melt into his kiss.

It's nice to know there is still honest to goodness love in the world. Bobbi Jo hoped they would always have that.

Carley waved to her husband as he drove away. Looking at her watch, she barked at the garage door, "Okay, peeping tom, you can stop eavesdropping, and get your ass out here. Fred's badgering, has put us behind schedule."

Straightening her face, Bobbi Jo opened the door and reversed her car out. Leaving the engine running, she secured the service bay, a little puzzled when she heard the trunk of the De Soto slam. Even more confused when she saw Carley behind the wheel.

"What gives?" Bobbi Jo jerked her head at the trunk. "And that's my seat."

"Picnic lunch," Carley countered cryptically. "And you drive too slow. Get in and buckle up."

Chapter Fourteen

Carley raced south to the Driller's oil field, hating to admit, the power in the DeSoto's Hemi engine was superior to her precious Wesa. At 5:25, they were on the access road leading to the main gate.

Pulling off at the bottom of the incline, Bobbi Jo was never supposed to climb, Carley parked so they were facing the traffic leaving the site. Checking the gas gauge, she left the vehicle idling.

Bobbi Jo, who had hardly spoken, decided to ask the question which had bothered her since they left the service station.

"Okay? What's going on? You had me travel this stupid road for a week, making sure no one saw me...a damn near impossible feat, I might add, never mind the gas I used...and now you're not going to let me drive?"

"Nah, I just did that to keep you out of the way so I could finish putting the pieces together. You'll understand when this is over."

A sporadic parade of cars began to crest the top of the

hill. In the cold, pre-dawn darkness it was difficult to judge the make and color as they cruised passed.

"Your plan won't work, Carley, there's too many cars traveling back into the city. We should just call it a day and go back to the drawing board."

Carley studied the stream of traffic, not dignifying her accomplice with a response.

"Do you even know what kind of car Clarence drives?" Bobbi Jo's nerves were telling her they were going to get caught.

As the line thinned out, a final car peaked the hill, made it down to the other side and slid passed them. A quick glance established the red lenses on both rear lights were broken, revealing the white bulbs — confirmation this was their target.

"A 1946 Oldsmobile...that one. Good job, Mac," Carley muttered.

"What, you got Mac involved in this, too? Christ, that's why I didn't want anybody to know. I made that mistake in St Louis. Too many people knew I was looking for—"

"For the love of God...shut the hell up," Carley exhorted.

She let the Oldsmobile get a short distance ahead, then engaged first gear, and spun the De Soto onto the road, kicking up a cloud of gravel behind her.

She focused on the broken taillights, using their illumination to navigate Bobbi Jo's car, refusing to turn on her own headlights.

Bobbi Jo closed her eyes and pressed her lips together as her nails sank into the dash, positive they were going to run off the road.

The big block Detroit engine under the hood of the

DeSoto brought it to the rear of the older car with hair-raising speed.

Clarence was silhouetted in glow from his dashboard and Carley caught the outline of his head when he lifted it to glance at the mirror.

Perfect timing... she switched on the headlights, the high beams flooding the Oldsmobile's interior.

Temporarily blinded by the reflection, in conjunction with the fatigue from his twelve hours in the field, Clarence lost control of the large car, which swerved wildly on the loose gravel.

Helping it along, Carley nudged the rear bumper hard enough to send it careening into the flat land beside the road.

Carley hit the brake, and the De Soto slewed to a halt. Unsure whether Clarence was injured, she leapt out and charged toward the Oldsmobile's door.

He had managed to unlatch it and was climbing out on wobbly legs. A thin line of blood trickled down his forehead.

"What the hell are you doing? Are you drunk or something?" He could not see who he was talking to, his vision distorted by the glare of headlights. "If you did any damage to my car, I'm gonna—"

"Shut your mouth and get on your knees," Carley commanded in stentorian tones, pulling her service .45 from the back of her jeans.

"Look, if you're some kind of wannabe highway robber, I can tell you you've got the wrong guy. I don't have two nickels to—"

"I told you to shut your mouth, otherwise I'll do it for you...permanently."

Observing the exchange, Bobbi Jo was not sure what was more disconcerting, that Carley had concealed an automatic pistol on her person without Bobbi Jo noticing, or how cool she was in a tense situation.

"Jo, don't forget the picnic lunch," Carley's gaze did not move from the enraged man in front of her. She heard the grass rustle as Clarence shifted his weight, alerting her to the fact he was thinking of doing something stupid. Cocking back the hammer, she warned, "Just you try it, ya bastard. If it were up to me I'd shoot you here, but my girl has other ideas."

Bobbi Jo was baffled. *Why the hell does Carley want lunch? What happened to breakfast? Wait... is she planning to force-feed Clarence his last meal?*

"Christ, don't tell me she's gonna give the son of a bitch a poisoned apple? What does she think this is, a frigging cartoon?" she groused under her breath.

Bobbi Jo's confusion fled when she popped the trunk of the De Soto. There, instead of some arsenic-laced buffet — two, well-used, garden shovels nestled on the blanket...*picnic lunch indeed.*

As she hefted one out, a grim smile curved her mouth at Carley's macabre sense of humour, which widened when she pictured Clarence's expression had she been able to conceal the implement until the last minute.

Regrettably, that was an impossibility, so — quashing *that* particular desire — she slung it, workmanlike, over her shoulder, and trudged to join them.

Standing scant feet from the man who had stalked her nightmares for the past few days, Bobbi Jo stared at him, wordlessly, knowing how this was going to end.

Carley leaned close. "Get the keys out of the ignition and open the trunk."

Bobbi Jo propped the spade against the Oldsmobile with a distinct *clang,* noting, with some satisfaction, Clarence wincing at the sound. To avoid any chance of their captive seizing her, unawares, she opted to do Carley's bidding from the passenger side.

Then she picked up the shovel, and stretched over to unlock the trunk, her eyes fixed on Carley, who nodded.

Bobbi Jo got into position behind Clarence.

Clarence's face was a mask of disbelief as he looked at the trunk then back at the pistol. "What do you think you're gonna do, bitch? Make me get in there? Not a fucking chance."

Carley had foreseen this scenario.

"Don't worry, asswipe, we thought you might feel that way."

Before Clarence could answer, Bobbi Jo had cracked the back of his head with the garden tool turned weapon.

The impact reverberated through Bobbi Jo, and made the stomach-wrenching sound she had *expected* to hear when she tried to bash in Roy's head. The actuality of metal fracturing bone was no less nauseating, made worse by the blood which splattered her as Clarence collapsed to the ground.

Barely conscious, Clarence felt the women struggle to get him to his feet. He tried to fight them off, but all that resulted in was a thwack to the side of his head with the pistol.

Stars danced in front of his eyes, dimming as the world around him went dark.

The last thing he heard was the clang of trunk lid dropping closed over him.

. . .

"Okay, Bobbi Jo, listen closely." Carley took the keys from the trunk. "I'm gonna drive his car and you're gonna follow me, understand?"

Mutely, Bobbi Jo nodded.

"Good, and whatever you do stay close behind me, do *not* let me get pulled over for broken tail lights. I spot flashing red lights, and you won't see me for dust. We're way beyond trying to explain why we have a guy in the trunk. If you *do* get stopped, I expect you to stall the troopers long enough for me to vanish."

Climbing into the Oldsmobile, Carley fired it up and nosed it back onto the road, making sure not to get stuck in the dirt.

In the time it took for Carley to pull in front of the DeSoto, Bobbi Jo was ready to go.

Looking to the eastern horizon, Bobbi Jo saw a hint of pearlescent gray breaking through the dark indigo of night. The undersides of the morning clouds were stained in a soft dusky pink. This breathtaking announcement assured her, the sunrise was imminent.

She exhaled a relieved sigh, counting the minutes until she could switch off her headlights, reducing the risk of being noticed by an overly diligent cop

The pair drove to Cherokee Nation territory.

Just over three hours later, they crossed into the reservation.

Turning off the highway, Carley followed the signs to

Duchess Landing. She knew this place well. Her dad had taken her fishing here when she was a child. Some of her happiest memories were of days spent on these banks.

She whispered a plea to her father's spirit, "Please forgive me for what I'm about to do in your favorite spot. We have no other choice."

The pounding from the trunk silenced any response she might have received from the great beyond.

Bringing the Oldsmobile to a halt, Carley alighted and, as the DeSoto cruised to a stop next to her, waited patiently for the motor to silence and the driver's side window to wind down.

"Are you ready?"

Bobbi Jo nodded and climbed out of her car.

Leaning into the backseat, she grabbed the spade and was about to fetch the other one from the trunk.

"You only need one, hun."

"A-Are we going to make him dig his own grave?" Bobbi Jo asked.

"No, doll, you are."

"*What?*" Bobbi Jo squeaked.

"If you intend to take a man's life, girl, you need to know what it's like to stand in his grave."

Leaving her to start digging, Carley returned to the Oldsmobile and turned up the volume on the radio to mute the cursing and shouts coming from the trunk.

Bobbi Jo felt as though she had been digging for the entire day. She considered herself in good shape but, after the first hour, her shoulders and back protested vigorously with each shovelful.

The handle of the spade was damp and dark from her blistered palms, and droplets of blood fell into the dirt, marking the place as hers.

Leaning against the shovel, Bobbi Jo paused to catch her breath. She looked at the hole she was standing in and realized it was barely above her knee.

Eyes lifted to Carley, who was standing over her smoking, holding the other spade.

"How much more do I have to dig?" she entreated, lamely.

Carley sighed and jumped down. "At least another foot or so, unless you want the coyotes to dig him up."

That was an alternative, Bobbi Jo could not tolerate. Neither bothered saying anything as they continued to dig.

It was not until groundwater began seeping into the bottom of the hole that Carley deemed it deep enough.

Carley gave Bobbi Jo a leg up, then stretched out her hand for the latter to return the favor, noting Bobbi Jo's expression bore the burden of someone learning what it means to commit murder.

With a tired grunt, Bobbi Jo hauled Carley out. Covered in mud and sweat, the two looked each other over.

Carley tossed her head toward the Oldsmobile. "Ready?"

Bobbi Jo went to the trunk and slid the key into its lock. Taking her place next to the side of the Oldsmobile as she had done before, she waited for Carley's signal.

Once in position, Carley nodded at Bobbi Jo who stretched over to unlatch the trunk.

Crazed from spending half the day in a tiny, dark,

almost airless space, dried blood clinging to the back of his head, Clarence lunged out, a tire iron clenched in his fists. He swung it wildly, uncaring which one he hit, swearing to kill both of them.

A bullet from Carley's gun burrowed through his shoulder, stinging like a motherfucker and he dropped the crude weapon.

Stumbling back against the vehicle, Clarence tried to retrieve the metal bar with his other hand, but Bobbi Jo beat him to the punch, snatching it away.

Carley ordered her accomplice, "Get over here."

No sooner had Bobbi Jo obeyed, than Carley gave her the gun. "It's your game now."

Clarence figured this was as good a time as any to charge them. He figured the girl could not hit the broad side of a barn. A poor choice on his part. He got two steps before Bobbi Jo put a bullet in his right kneecap, bringing him down like a rampaging buffalo.

"Drag your sorry ass over to the hole," she snapped.

"Why?" Clarence begged. "Why are you doing this to me? I don't know either one of you bitches."

"If you want me to spare your life, get into the hole."

Bleeding, and experiencing the kind of pain he imagined his brother, Daryl, had felt when the liquor store owner shot him, he crawled toward the pit.

"Please, whatever I did to you two, please forgive me. Just drop me off at the hospital and I swear I won't report you. I'll tell them my gun backfired," he bleated.

When he reached the hole, Clarence could not bring himself to drop over the edge, only to feel two sets of hands push him in. He hit the soggy bottom headfirst.

Rolling to his back, Clarence looked up at the cloud

laden sky. The women's faces came into focus as they glared down at him.

"Who are you?"

He saw the pair glance across the grave at each other, they shared an expression of hatred he could not fathom.

Finally, the younger one spoke, "You're right, you don't know me, at least me as I am now, but you *did* know a five year old girl who witnessed you and your brother kill her family, then leave her for dead in a blizzard. Ring any bells?"

Clarence's eyes grew wide. "N-No. There's no way you could have survived that snow storm."

"So you *do* remember," Bobbi Jo's features softened into the semblance of a smile.

"How did you track me down? And why?"

"Stupid questions. I'm here because you sent Roy — remember Roy? — a letter pleading for him to come save you. Did you really think he would?

"As for why? This is where I decide your appropriate justice. You know...whether you live or die. All you have to do is tell me where I can find Buchanan."

"Buchanan? H-How the hell would I know? He skipped town owing me money. I have no idea—"

Bobbi Jo bummed one of Carley's cigarettes as Clarence gabbled on. Lighting the smoke, she gave Clarence a shrug and the two of them stepped back.

This time it was not Bobbi Jo's mom who whispered in her mind. This time it was Jimmy's voice she heard urging her, "Do it, Bobbi Jo. Drop the match. He deserves it."

With a nod, she flicked it into the grave. The glow of the match seemed to intensify as it fluttered downwards, reminiscent of a firefly.

Clarence tried to avoid it, but his wounds made it impossible.

The small flame touched the crude oil soaked into the fabric of his shirt, bursting into a rolling blaze.

In agony, Clarence screamed for help, promising to tell them anything they wanted to hear. Unfortunately for him, his words fell on deaf ears.

His cries were drowned out by the roar of the inferno engulfing him. His swift demise, inevitable.

Black smoke billowed up for no one to see, its isolation the very reason Carley had chosen this spot.

As the clouds began to disperse, the pair started to refill the hole. When the first shovelful hit what remained of Clarence's face, Bobbi Jo delivered a cursory homily, "Roy is waiting in hell for you. I hope you have whatever money you owe him."

They finished burying Clarence, then Bobbi Jo followed Carley to an auto salvage yard in the heart of the reservation.

After they drove through the gate, it was closed by the owner, an older Cherokee named Wahali, who led them to a large barn.

Inside, Bobbi Jo spotted a number of vehicles in various stages of disassembly. She had already discussed the fate of the De Soto she had, begrudgingly, grown to love.

Carley abandoned Clarence's Oldsmobile like it was radioactive. Opening Bobbi Jo's door, she said. "It's time to go."

"How? You're gonna kill my car."

Giving her a smile, Carley whistled at Wahali.

The old man walked over, dangled a key in front of Bobbi Jo's nose, and swept an ancient hand at the side exit.

Like a bratty older sister, Carley snatched the key and ran outside.

Before Bobbi Jo caught up, she heard the rumble of an engine. Stepping through the door, she discovered Carley sitting behind the wheel of a 1954 Hudson Hornet.

The body of the car might be scuffed and beaten, and its one-time gleaming black paint had long since faded to charcoal, but its 7-X engine purred like it did the day it rolled off the Kenosha, Wisconsin assembly line.

Revving the engine a few times, Carley let it tick over as she opened the door and scooted over for Bobbi Jo to get behind the wheel.

She beamed, "I know she doesn't look like much, but Wahali used to race this baby on the dirt tracks. She's unbeatable...and lovingly cared for."

"I-I don't understand. What is this for?" Bobbi Jo asked, feeling the power of the car as her fingers curled around the steering wheel.

Through the mirror, she saw the old man placing her belongings from the DeSoto into the Hudson's trunk.

As suddenly as he had appeared, he was gone.

"Consider this my severance package. You're fired, by the way, and I don't ever want to see you in Oklahoma City again. Don't bother arguing...or I'll personally hand you over to the tribal cops. You just murdered a man on reservation lands meaning it falls to their jurisdiction and nobody else's.

Bobbi Jo bit her lip contemplating the validity of Carley's threat.

Carley added, "Did I happen to mention my cousin is the Tribal Police Chief?"

Thinking it wiser to change topics, Bobbi Jo queried "But won't that put you in a bind at the café? I mean this car can't be cheap...and, well, won't your niece be returning to college soon?"

Bobbi Jo had been puzzled when the girl didn't go back at the end of August.

"Don't worry about the café. Seems the real reason Eddie came home is because one of her professors put a bun in her oven. She won't be going back to California anytime soon...if ever."

Out of the blue, another thought struck Bobbi Jo. "Carley...what about the dog?"

"Dog?" Jokingly, Carley pressed the back of her hand to Bobbi Jo's forehead. "Nope, no fever. What dog?"

"Clarence has a dog...big, huge, enormous doberman. Scary as all get out, but the mutt doesn't deserve to starve to death because his owner is a douche-bag."

Carley patted her knee in a motherly fashion. "Don't fret, I'll sort it... an anonymous call to animal control should the trick. Hmm," she mused, "Fred could do with a guard dog..."

Bobbi Jo chuckled. "You are such a softy."

"Wash your mouth out. Right, enough of this sentimental claptrap. The day's a wastin'."

There was a pause as the two women looked at each other.

"I don't know how to thank you." An unfamiliar wave of sadness rippled through Bobbi Jo.

"Well, taking me to my mom's place would be a good start, I'll get a ride home from there." Carley grinned, lightening the mood. "Other than that, not getting caught finding Buchanan will be enough. Oh, and make sure to check the glove compartment once you are well outside the state."

"Yes, ma'am," Bobbi Jo swallowed a sob and drew Carley into a fierce hug.

Blinking back tears, she straightened up and drove out of the yard.

Chapter Fifteen

Meeting Carley's mother was a profound, if brief, encounter for Bobbi Jo whose intention was to drop Carley off and scarper. The latter and her mother had other ideas.

An older version of her daughter, save her fathomless dark eyes, the Cherokee woman seemed to see right inside her.

Upon being introduced, she cupped Bobbi Jo's face, brushing her thumb over the barely perceptible scars. "Do not let these define or consume you. You have survived what would have defeated most, yet your chosen path remains torturous.

Your sprit is torn and your soul restless. The peace you crave is within your grasp, but currently veiled by your hatred, your quest to settle a score." She tilted her head and dropped her hand.

"Oh, child... I pity and admire you. There are two beasts with opposing emotions at war in your heart, and the victor will be the one you feed."

Stunned by the woman's almost prophetic words, Bobbi

Jo who had paled to a sickly ashen hue, was unable to articulate a response, if one was even expected.

She shot a despairing glance at Carley who held her
gaze for several seconds before nodding slowly.

No more was said and the conversation moved onto
lighter subjects, but Bobbi Jo was uncomfortable under so
shrewd a regard. Although sad to say goodby to Carley, as
soon as she deemed it polite, she made her excuses and,
citing a long journey, left.

Once beyond the jurisdiction of the reservation, Bobbi Jo
stopped the car to study the map she had bought at the
service station in Oklahoma City.

She calculated that the half-way point to Truckee, California would take seventeen hours by car. Despite how
desperately she wanted to drive straight through to Las
Vegas, to attempt it would doubtless end in disaster.

The Hudson had decent gas mileage for a car its size,
but the fact it dwarfed her dearly departed DeSoto meant
more breaks to refuel, and she prayed they wouldn't become
too frequent.

Her first stop came at a dot of a town near the border
between Texas and New Mexico. Bobbi Jo cursed herself
for not filling up in Amarillo, but was positive the car could
make the distance, and she hadn't been hungry at that
point.

It made for a harrowing seventy-two mile experience.
Once past Adrian, Texas, she swore the needle on the gas
gauge buried itself below E.

True to Carley's faith in Wahali's mechanical skills, the

Hornet rolled into Glenrio, New Mexico without so much as a sputter of an empty tank.

Spotting a two-pump gas station, she was happy to let the attendant fill her beast — with premium no less.

Vital fluids checked and topped, she carried on to the next truck stop, not far ahead. About to climb out of the car, Bobbi Jo remembered Carley's cryptic parting instruction. This remote corner of the world seemed as good a place as any to check the glovebox.

Opening it, she found an envelope and Carley's .45 inside. She guessed the gun was given not only as a source of protection, but also to get rid of the evidence should Clarence ever be found.

Still, it comforted Bobbi Jo to know Carley was still watching out for her in her own way.

She slid out the envelope. Flipping it over, she read — in Carley's distinctive scrawl — *Happy Birthday!*

Perplexed, Bobbi Jo muttered, "It's not my birthday."

Slitting the flap with her nail, she peeked inside. It held a bundle of cash, a note, and something which looked like official papers. Bobbi Jo stuffed everything into her purse and went into the truck stop.

Before she found a booth, she made a personal pitstop. The last thirty miles had played havoc with her kidneys.

Making herself comfortable at a table, Bobbi Jo watched a cute brunette waitress dance her way to Bobbi Jo's table to the rhythm of whatever song was blaring from the jukebox.

Cheerfully, the woman took the order for a sandwich and a pop.

Bobbi Jo's lips twitched in amusement as she watched the waitress bebop her way into the kitchen, wondering whether the woman had actually heard the request.

With a shrug she turned her attention back to the envelope and its contents. Sliding everything out, she unfolded the note and began to read.

Jo,

I wish we could have parted under better circumstances, but things happen for a reason, I guess.

Anyway, find enclosed your last pay. I know it ain't much, but I hope it covers gas and expenses to California.

I also know, had I tried to hand it to you, you would have turned it down. So, blame yourself for all the subterfuge.

Likewise, in the envelope, you should find an Oklahoma driver's license and registration for the car.

Since you pick the worst aliases, I claimed the privilege of naming you, Miss Charlotte Bernhard.

You'll think this is hokey, but Charlotte means a free man. And you are definitely close to being free from your past.

I thought about blessing you with a Cherokee family name...but I'm afraid you can't pull it off, and my ancestors would probably strike both of us dead.

I did consider my choice carefully, though.

Bernhard is German and means 'as strong and as brave as a bear.' And you, my girl, you truly do have the heart of a bear.

Well, you're about to arrive, so I'll close here. Stay safe and know there are people praying for you.

Love, Carley

Bobbi Jo looked at the license and registration. They stated the owner of the Hudson resided in Tulsa, a place she had buzzed through on the way to Oklahoma City and that, as of yesterday, she was twenty-two. The girl chuckled to see she was *officially* of age.

Neatly folding all the papers, she replaced them in her

purse in time to see the plate with her sandwich appear in front of her.

Thanking the waitress, Bobbi Jo devoured her meal and, shortly thereafter was back on the road.

The trip across New Mexico ended with a flat tire outside the small town of Gallup. Fortunately, a concerned motorist happened upon her, stranded on the side of the road.

The man wanted to prove that chivalry was alive and well.

While she appreciated the help, his endless conversations about knights and damsels in distress put her an hour behind schedule.

With a freshly patched spare and a full tank of gas, Bobbi Jo crossed the border into Arizona. Determined to make up time driving through the desert, she put her foot down.

As though waiting for the opportunity to show its prowess, the Hudson growled in response, and before Bobbi Jo realized, the speedometer was passing 100 mph.

She recouped the lost time rapidly but, when the gathering dusk darkened the desert sky, she slowed to a more appropriate speed.

High beams on, she rolled into Seligman, and the final fill-up for both her car and her stomach.

It was around two in the morning when Bobbi Jo reached the edge of the Vegas Strip. Even at this time of the night, the road was illuminated by the glare from millions of neon bulbs advertising the various casinos located along the stretch of desert road.

Ignoring the numerous flashy hotels, Bobbi Jo opted for an older, nondescript motel at the other end of the Strip.

Coming to a halt outside the office of the Golden Coin, Bobbi Jo, pried herself out of the Hudson and stretched, hearing her joints crack. Tired from the long drive, all she wanted to do was sleep.

After checking and locating her room, she did exactly that, the moment her head hit the pillow.

The next morning, Bobbi Jo decided to leave her car at the motel, and walk to the city center. She was astonished at how many people were wandering the Strip at such an early hour, just to gamble, their grizzled expressions indicating none had yet been to sleep.

The invitations to free buffets for those gambling enticed the girl in.

At first, she started out on the slot machines. With the self-promise of not losing more than a couple of dollars, Bobbi Jo played the penny slots. It was not long before she grew tired of winning and losing the same twenty-five cents.

From there, she wandered over to the roulette table and stood next to a guy in a cowboy hat watching him play. He seemed to be winning, though not a lot.

As the little white ball dropped into seventeen black, the man began to hoot and holler. On a ten dollar bet, he won three hundred and fifty dollars.

He glanced at Bobbi Jo as he raked in his chips, giving her a broad smile. "Well, I'll be danged if it ain't Lady Luck come to visit my table."

Bobbi Jo looked around her to see who the man was talking about but, aside from the two of them, she could only see the croupier.

She blushed at the compliment. "I think you got the wrong woman."

"Really," he teased, "how about we put that to the test?"

He handed her a ten dollar chip.

"Pick a number."

Bobbi Jo studied the wheel intently, then placed the chip on her chosen square. "Thirteen Black."

"Thirteen Black it is," he repeated to the croupier.

The croupier spun the wheel clockwise before sending the ball in the opposite direction.

While Bobbi Jo thought it an exercise in futility, she was beside herself when the tiny ball dropped into thirteen.

The cowboy nudged her shoulder as the croupier paid her the same three hundred and fifty he had just paid the cowboy, who proceeded to teach her different ways to win.

By the third win, Bobbi Jo was hooked and asked the cowboy, "Sir, where can I get my own chips?"

Following his direction, she exchanged a hundred for chips. She reasoned, with two hundred she could stay in a better class of hotel, and not worry about food or gas.

That was when her luck ran out.

Bobbi Jo lost everything she had won for the cowboy, and then the money Carley had given her

The cowboy urged her on, persuading her that all she had to do was place one more bet.

Placing a couple of chips on twenty-four and black, she did not see her new 'friend' palm the rest of her chips and disappear into the throng of gamblers.

When the marble dropped into the five red slot alongside her bet, common sense reasserted itself. She had lost enough. Reaching for her remaining chips, she was stunned to realize they, and her friend, had gone.

Leaning on the table, she lifted up onto her tiptoes in an effort to spot him and his gaudy hat in the crowd.

The croupier chided, "Miss, please do not upset the table."

Bobbi Jo babbled, "Where's the cowboy gone? He was right here a second ago?"

"Miss, this is a huge casino. I have no idea where he went."

"But my chips...he stole them."

"Happens if you don't pay attention. Want me to call Security?"

"Will it do me any good?"

The croupier shrugged in sympathetic resignation.

Pissed off, Bobbi Jo marched out of the casino, and back to the motel.

Sitting in the front seat of her car, she counted what was left in her purse. The grand total was a little over a hundred and a half.

Disgusted with humanity...and herself, Bobbi Jo fled the city as quickly as she could. Stopping in Corn Creek long enough to fill her tank, she looked back at the glitter of Las Vegas and swore, "I've served my time in Hell. I have no need to visit it again."

From there, she drove onto Mina, Nevada. The place was not much larger than Corn Creek, which suited Bobbi Jo fine. It took her mere minutes for her to top the tank and grab the cheapest meal she could manage.

The stop cost her a total of twelve dollars. At this stage, she needed to count every penny she had left. She knew once she reached Truckee, a hundred dollars was not going to last long between food and rent.

Bobbi Jo chewed over how to eke out her money. Hopefully, she might be lucky enough to find a bar or restaurant in need of a waitress.

Putting that on the back burner, she concentrated on driving. The desert scenery was magnificent and, had she possessed the time, would have pulled to the side of the road and savored it.

An indulgence for another day.

Burying the accelerator, she covered the distance from Mina to Reno in just over two hours.

Coasting into the 'Biggest Little City in the World', Bobbi Jo wound down the window and spat on the road.

She already hated everything about the place.

It had allowed those scumbags to abscond from its jail and go on the run. Their determination to escape, culminating in the murder of her family.

As far as she could tell, its police force had made no effort during the intervening years to apprehend *any* of the bastards.

Bobbi Jo remembered standing in her bedroom, her mother's dried blood stippling the wall, listening to men in uniform talk about how much credence would be given to evidence provided by a five year old.

The only thing she had been able to tell them were four names, which the authorities suspected were aliases.

Even if the perpetrators were arrested, the girl would make a lousy witness. Any slick lawyer worth his salt would make her crumble under cross-examination and get them off in a heartbeat.

Nevertheless, Bobbi Jo parked the Hudson outside the police station. Swallowing the bile in her throat, she gathered her dignity along with her purse, and entered the building.

The desk sergeant looked up from his newspaper to see a slip of a girl standing in front of his desk.

Giving her a once over, he saw no physical marks on her, nor was she acting hysterically, which suggested she was not there to file a report.

Half-heartedly, he grumbled, "How may I help you, miss?"

Bobbi Jo cleared her throat and announced, "My name is Charlotte Bernhard. I'm majoring in journalism here in Reno and I am writing a paper on unsolved crimes in the area. Do you have any detectives available to whom I could talk regarding a jail break which occurred here in the fifties?"

The desk sergeant sighed and yelled over his shoulder, "Sheriff Pitmann, you have company."

Sheriff Virgil Pittman was a product of a bygone era. With his bushy gray mustache, perched above his pudgy upper lip, he looked as though he would be more comfortable in 1864 than 1964.

He rose to his booted feet when Bobbi Jo entered his office. Extending his arm, he invited her to take a seat.

Lighting a cigar, he asked through the smoke, "How can this old cowboy be of help to a pretty young thing like you?"

"Well, you can start," Bobby Jo replied disdainfully, "by addressing me properly. It's Ms. Bernhard."

Pitmann set his cigar in the ashtray on his desk and studied the girl for a moment.

"Well, *Ms.* Bernhard, I'm not sure what fancy city you came from, but it is clear manners were not part of your formal education."

Leaning back in his swivel chair, he flapped a meaty hand at the collection of rifles mounted on the wall behind him.

Bobbi Jo could not help but look at them. They were various makes and gauges.

Pitmann explained, "Over the last forty-odd years of public service, each of these rifles was discharged in the line of duty, bringing a criminal before their maker for their ultimate justice.

"I am of the firm belief none of those men had been taught how to be polite either. So, should we try this little meet and greet again?"

Reprimanded by the very man down whose throat she wanted to ram that putrid cigar, Bobbi Jo bit back her instinctive reply, deciding discretion was the better part of valor.

"I apologize, sir. My name is Charlotte Bernhard, and I am studying journalism at college. If it would not be too much of an inconvenience, may I ask for information for a paper I am writing?"

The entire introduction was like chewing rocks.

"I'll be happy to help anyway I can." Pitmann reclaimed his cigar and took a puff. "What on earth is it about our office that has piqued your curiosity sufficiently to dedicate one page to, never mind a whole paper? Parking tickets on Main Street? Halloween vandals?"

"No, sir. An unsolved escape from your jail in 1952.

Four men killed a couple of deputies and kidnapped one, later killing him too."

"Why would you be interested in ancient history? Anyway, you got your facts wrong. The case was closed by the FBI spring of the same year."

"Excuse me? The case was closed?"

"Yeah, J. Edgar's boys came over from 'Frisco and poked around for a few days. They concluded the escapees must have frozen to death in the blizzard. There was no way they could have gotten anywhere once they abandoned the car."

"B-But what about the murders on Donner Pass?"

Pitmann shrugged, rocking back in his chair. He exhaled a cloud of smoke which coiled above him.

"The Feds deemed the case unrelated. They went through the house with a fine tooth comb, and couldn't find anything to put those boys there when it happened.

"Anway, them folks were shot with a scatter gun and none of the four was armed with one."

Bobbi Jo's mouth dropped open in disbelief.

"And because of that flimsy evidence you geniuses came up with the conclu—"

"Now you wait there, missy," Pitmann barked, rising from his chair. "The cases were thoroughly investigated by professionals, here and in California. You have no business dredging up the past with baseless accusations.

"If I can give you a bit of advice. Go back to that fancy campus of yours and ask your professor for another topic, maybe one about cooking the perfect Thanksgiving dinner."

"I won't let you minimize my concerns about the lack of actual policing any of you have done in twelve years. Do you not care about finding justice for the little girl who was left an orphan because of the tragedy?"

Irritated by the woman's attitude, Pitmann rounded the

desk without warning. Thick fingers grasped Bobbi Jo gently, but firmly, and lifted her out of her seat.

He chastised, "From what I remember of the girl, she ended up with a good family somewhere out east. I'm sure she's living a happy life and has no need of the likes of you causing her any problems."

Giving Bobbi Jo no chance to argue, Pitmann escorted her to his office door.

Opening it, he pushed her out. "I recommend you let sleeping dogs lie. Reno has a small town attitude, and poking into things you know nothing about could lead to people getting their feelings hurt. Good day, Ms. Bernhard."

Before Bobbi Jo could stop him, he slammed his office door shut.

Conceding she had hit a dead end, Bobbi Jo stomped out of the station and climbed into the Hudson. Infuriated, she decided it was time to head to the only sure lead she had...Truckee, California.

Chapter Sixteen

To save a few dollars, Bobbi Jo opted to find a boarding house instead of a motel. Spending a dime on the local paper, she searched the classifieds while sipping a cup of coffee at a truck-stop outside Truckee.

As she flipped through the paper, the waitress who was refilling her cup tilted her head to see what the girl was reading.

"New in town, Toots?" the woman chirped.

Bobbi Jo looked up at her, slightly annoyed at being interrupted. "Yeah, just got in."

"Really? Are you traveling through or thinking of staying for a bit?"

"Kinda stranded, I guess," Bobbi Jo admitted to the waitress, who joined her in the booth.

"Stranded? How?"

"Um, shouldn't you be working?" Bobbi Jo quizzed.

"Does it look busy in here? Besides, it's not every day I get to talk to a new resident with a story. What do you mean by stranded?"

Aware she was not going to get rid of the woman any other way, Bobbi Jo explained about the incident in Vegas.

The woman shook her head in dismay. "How awful, you certainly can't trust people these days. Do you have enough money to stay anywhere? If not I know of a place—"

"Oh, no you don't. I don't need to make a living in the world's oldest profession."

The waitress cocked her head, "What the hell are you talking about? Jesus, I've never been accused of that before. I was only going to suggest checking out McGuire's boarding house. It's cheap and clean."

Blushing at misjudging the woman, Bobbi Jo said contritely, "I'm sorry. I'm just on edge. This trip has been one continuous nightmare. This boarding house, is it close?"

"It's a couple of blocks over on Donner. Big sign outside the place."

The man in the kitchen yelled through the window, "Ginny, get your ass in gear and get this food out. It won't serve itself."

"You sure, Bud? I think I saw your prime rib barrel racing at the rodeo grounds."

"Zip your lip and get back to work before I fire you."

"I should be so lucky," the waitress shot back. Returning her attention to the girl, she said, "Tell, Mrs. McGuire, Ginny sent you. Should put you on the ins with her. She serves some of the best food this side of the Sierras."

"Thanks, I'll check her out."

"By the way, hun, what's your name? I told you mine, seems only fair I know yours."

"Dammit, Ginny, the food is getting cold."

"It was cold in the can you just opened, Bud, another minute won't kill it...though it might be good if it did."

Bobbi Jo laughed at the banter. "I'm Charlotte Bernhard, but everybody calls me Charlie."

"Nice to meet you, Charlie. Come back when you get settled in."

"Thank you, Ginny. I appreciate your help, and I will. Now you better get to work."

The Hudson rolled up the gravel drive to a large three-story, white-washed house. As per Ginny's description, the large sign in the yard proclaimed proudly,

The McGuires' Retreat
All Are Welcome
As long as you pay in cash
In Advance

There was additional stuff written beneath in even smaller print, but straining her eyes to read it gave Bobbi Jo a headache. She figured if it was important the owners would tell her.

Alighting from the car, she followed the path through a side gate which matched the white picket fence. The lawn and garden were meticulously kept. Even in the midst of fall, there were still roses to be seen.

Climbing the steps, she crossed the porch, complete with a lovers' swing and rocking chairs, to the front door. She smoothed her dress out before knocking.

Tapping on the beveled stained glass, Bobbi Jo took a step back to wait for an answer.

Through the pane, she saw a hazy outline approaching.

When the door opened, Bobbi Jo was met by an older woman who she swore was Mrs. Claus in disguise. Her cherub face was graced with a welcoming smile. Her snow white hair swept up into a grandmotherly bun.

The woman greeted brightly, "Welcome to McGuire's Boarding House. How may I help you, my dear?"

"Mrs. McGuire? Ginny from the café—"

The mere mention of the waitress's name caused a scowl to furrow Mother Christmas's brow.

The door banged shut, and the woman yelled, "If you're friends with that delinquent, tell her she still owes me two days' rent and I want my autographed picture of Frankie back."

"M-Mrs. McGuire...I only met her a few minutes ago, and guarantee, I don't know what's going on between the two of you. All I'd like to know is whether you have a room available?"

Adding, "I have cash."

The door opened a crack. Mrs. McGuire demanded suspiciously, "Let me see."

Bobbi Jo dug through her purse and produced her handful of remaining bills. As if the money had sprung the door's lock, it opened wide, the old woman wiping her hands on her apron.

"The rent is a dollar a day...two if you're expecting breakfast and dinner. Lunch is your responsibility. I am not running a restaurant here after all. As the sign clearly states, gentleman callers are only allowed on the porch...during the daytime hours. This ain't no brothel either."

"Thank God for that," Bobbi Jo mumbled.

"What was that, girl? Speak up when you talk."

"I said, thank God you have a respectable place."

Giving Bobbi Jo a dubious look, Mrs. McGuire went on, "Most importantly, all tenants are required to attend church with us every Sunday. No exceptions."

"Excuse me? You require the people staying here to go to church with you? Have they all complied?"

"If they want to stay here...yes."

Bobbi Jo wondered whether she should ask the next question, but curiosity trumped discretion. "By the way, how many people *are* staying with you?"

"Well, things are a little slow right now. So if you take a room...that will make two."

"Two?" Bobbi Jo was incredulous.

"Yes, you...and..." Mrs. McGuire was hesitant to say, but there was no way back, "...and that hussy Ginny."

Falling silent for a moment, Bobbi Jo pressed, "If she's such a troublesome tenant, why don't you ask her to leave?"

"How could you expect me to kick out my own grand-daughter? What kind of person do you take me for?"

Before Bobbi Jo could offer a reasoned evaluation, Mrs. McGuire held out her hand. "I expect thirty days up front, and is that your car in my drive?" She waved her other hand at the Hudson.

"Y-Yes, ma'am."

"You better move it. No one is allowed to park there. That space is reserved for Mr. McGuire's fancy white Rambler station wagon. If he finds your car there...ever...he will have it towed."

"Where am I supposed to park then?" Bobbi Jo asked, mildly agitated at the blatant threat.

"There are spaces in the alley for tenants' cars. So do you still want to see a room?"

"Yeah." The girl began to peel the money from the bundle. "Here's sixty. Please don't burn my toast."

The old woman snorted. "What did you say your name was again?"

"It's Charlotte Bernhard, but you can call me Charlie."

"Girls wanting boys names nowadays," the woman bemoaned as she led her new tenant up the stairs. "Why, in my day, we would not have thought of doing something so uncouth."

Mrs. McGuire's rant was replaced by another voice, this one in her head.

"You've done well, poppet. All that remains is to get Buchanan."

Mrs. McGuire gave Bobbi Jo the grand tour of the house, stipulating, "Our room is here on the second floor. I do not expect anyone on this floor after nine pm, disturbing us."

"Yes, ma'am," Bobbi Jo agreed.

Reaching the third floor, the old woman stopped to gesture at the flamboyantly decorated door to their right.

"That's Ginny's room," she explained, adding gruffly, "That is when she deems us worthy of her presence."

She opened the doors to the other three rooms allowing her new tenant to choose which suited her. Bobbi Jo couldn't really tell the difference. They were spacious and appeared comfortably furnished. Each contained a double bed, a wardrobe, and a cheval mirror mounted in an oak frame.

She settled on the one opposite Ginny's. It faced the

rear of the house, overlooking the back yard, as well as the alley and the neighbor's property beyond.

While the room did not have outside access, the fire door which led to the back staircase, was close enough that she could come and go without disturbing anyone. Her only concern was running into Ginny at an odd hour in the morning.

After carrying her suitcase up the endless stairs, Bobbi Jo decided to spend the remainder of the day looking for a job to tide her over until her task was completed.

Since there was only one business she knew of in Truckee, she descended the rear stairs and returned to her car.

It was time to visit Butterman's Storage.

Squatting at the edge of town, on the highway leading to the mountains, Butterman's Shipping and Storage was a sprawling, two-story, brick building.

In faded lettering on the side…Buchanan's Mercantile.

Bobbi Jo found *that* historical tidbit fascinating.

Entering the building, she was confronted with dust and the aroma of old things left in storage for too long.

Bobbi Jo approached the counter and tapped on the grubby surface. A decision she regretted, the index finger of her brand-new, white glove now stained a dull gray.

Fighting the urge to wipe it on her dress, she sighed internally. *That was a waste of a quarter*.

Clearing her throat, Bobbi Jo attempted to attract the attention of the man who had paid her no mind since she opened the door.

Tired of being ignored, Bobbi Jo piped up, perhaps a little louder than necessary, "Excuse me, may I get some help?"

The man glanced her way, stretching as he rose from his chair. "Yes, Miss, how may I be of assistance?"

"I'd like to check out one of your storage areas. I have some furniture I don't have room for currently, but don't want to throw away."

The man closed one eye and scrutinized her. "Ya seem a bit young for that kind of problem. Could it be you're trying to hide an ugly chair your husband can't give up?"

"I beg your pardon?" Bobbi Jo retorted, offended by the man's inference. "I'll have you know I am neither married nor dependent on a man. All I want is to rent a space. If that's too hard to fathom, I can go elsewhere." A hollow threat given this was probably the only storage place in town.

The old man chuckled, not bothering to apologize for his observation. "If you're still interested, I have a couple of units on the second floor. If you come this way, I'll be happy to show you."

Grabbing a set of keys, he steered her to a wooden lift. Opening the gate, he stepped out of the way allowing Bobbi Jo to precede him. Following behind, he closed the gate and inserted the key into the control switch, activating the electric motor above them.

As the machine crackled to life, Bobbi Jo looked at the man in concern.

He shrugged and pressed the UP button. "The old girl hasn't failed yet."

Bobbi Jo rolled her eyes, muttering, "There's always a first time."

The elevator ground its way to the dark second floor, where the manager floundered for the switch. A lucky smack ignited row upon row of fluorescent tubes, illuminating crates, boxes, and furniture in various stalls. Some were covered with sheets; others were exposed to the elements. All needed a good dusting.

"How big a space do you need?" The man asked, running a hand through his graying beard.

"I'm thinking enough for four or five crates and a couch."

"So a small one. Gotcha."

He led Bobbi Jo past rows of filled stalls. She had hoped the owners' names were posted on the gates, disappointed when she saw only numbers.

The old man stopped at a unit squeezed between over-stuffed ones. "Something like this?"

Bobbi Jo studied the space. "That might work, I'll have to think about it."

"Your call." He turned back toward the lift. "If it's still available once you've decided, it's yours for ten dollars a month.

"If I was you, I wouldn't wait too long though. Most of the cabins along the pass close up for the winter, and people want to keep their stuff protected until spring.

"It's supposed to be another nasty winter. Not as bad as the winters of '31 or '52, mind you, but still a lot of snow."

Returning her to the ground floor, the old man resumed his seat behind the counter, without another word.

Nonplussed, Bobbi Jo studied him. She had never met anyone so apathetic about his job. Then again, working in an environment like this was hardly a basis for boundless enthusiasm.

Prepared to leave him to his solitude, she noticed a sign

pinned to the corkboard next to the exit. A quick scan of the ad, and she snatched it off the board, retracing her steps to the counter.

Slapping the paper down, she spun it around so the old man could see it, jabbing on the words *Help Wanted*, with her dirty finger, leaving a smudge.

"Is this job still available?"

"Oh, Lord. That thing has been up there for years. I'd forgotten about it."

"That's all fine and dandy, but the question remains, are you still looking for help?"

"Why do you know a guy who needs a job? It doesn't pay—"

"I am asking for myself. I'd like to apply for the position."

"Come now, girly, you don't want this job. I think the supermarket might be looking for a cash—"

"Look, Mister, I'm a lot stronger than you think and from what I can see of this place, it could use a woman's touch."

"You do realize you will have to lug crates and shit. Likewise, you'll get dirty and sweaty by the end of the day. This is no fancy dress establishment."

"Good, I prefer overalls. Yes or no."

"What the hell. I daresay, you'll quit within a week anyway. A little help with inventory couldn't hurt. Be here tomorrow morning at eight, and be ready to work."

Bobbi Jo saluted the man and smiled. "Dressed and looking forward to proving myself."

Back in her car, she drove to the feed store to purchase overalls, several long-sleeved flannel shirts, and a pair of sturdy work boots.

At the boarding house, she washed her purchases and

tossed them into Mrs. McGuire's brand new clothes dryer without her permission so she would be ready for the next day.

Sometime in the middle of the night, squeaking floorboards outside her bedroom door, accompanied by a solid thud on the other side of her wall, roused Bobbi Jo from a deep slumber.

Staring up at the ceiling, she listened to the sounds of two sets of feet tiptoeing awkwardly across the hall. Bobbi Jo pressed her lips together to contain her laughter as she heard the steps stumble again, followed by smothered giggles and shushes.

She crept to her door and, cracking it wide enough to peek through, saw Ginny trying to secrete a man into her room.

Even the gloom could not hide the fact, the couple was drunk and, given Ginny's dishevelled appearance, had already been in the throes of foreplay before entering the house.

Bobbi Jo spotted Ginny's shoes clutched in her hand, and hoped her fellow tenant had discarded them *prior* to climbing the back stairs.

Ginny's companion towered over her and, while she struggled to open her door, lolled against her to fondle her butt, which earned him a solid smack.

Bobbi Jo heard Ginny's whispered admonishment, "Wait until we get inside."

Grinning at the ridiculous scene, she retreated into her room and shut the door softly.

The almost inaudible click prompted Ginny to shoot a quick glance over her shoulder. An impish smile twitched at her lips. She was going to enjoy sharing the floor with Charlie.

Chapter Seventeen

Before sunrise, Bobbi Jo was up and ready for her first day of work. Padding down the stairs, she found Mrs. McGuire in the kitchen.

The old woman greeted Bobbi Jo with a bright smile. Mr. McGuire said nothing, choosing to concentrate on his breakfast and morning paper.

Setting a plate of eggs and bacon in front of their new tenant, Mrs. McGuire smacked her taciturn husband on the back of his head.

"Winston, get your nose out of that fish wrapper and say good morning."

The beleaguered man dropped his paper at the fold line, to mumble, "Morning."

Mrs. McGuire poured herself a cup of coffee and joined them at the table. As she took a sip, she noticed how the girl was dressed.

"What are you planning to do today?" She was stuck by a horrifying thought. "Oh, my Lord. Don't tell me, you saw weeds in my garden yesterday and felt a burning desire to tend to them? How about I join you. You'll find the tools—"

Bobbi Jo broke in to reassure Mrs. McGuire, "Oh no, ma'am, your garden speaks volumes for your green thumb. I am dressed for work."

"Heavens, girl. What kind of job did you get? Picking vegetables?"

Bobbi Jo chuckled, "Nothing as drastic, ma'am. I got a job at Butterman's. I start this morning."

"Whatever possessed you to apply for a job with that derelict?"

"Roosevelt," Mr. McGuire blurted out. "If it wasn't for him and that damned New Deal garbage he foisted on America, women would have stayed home where they belong."

"Oh, Winston McGuire, shut your yap," his wife barked. "Nobody asked for your opinion."

He huffed and finished his breakfast.

Both women watched him bolt from his chair and out through the back door, letting it shut with a loud rattle. The drone of his car firing up announced he would not be back until day's end.

Taking another sip, Mrs. McGuire muttered, "Men."

Bobbi Jo looked at the clock. It was already 7:30. She dabbed her mouth with the pristine napkin. "If you will excuse me, Mrs. McGuire, I will be on my way as well."

"Just watch yourself around that reprobate," Mrs. McGuire warned.

"I think I can handle him." Bobbi Jo smiled.

"And I hope my granddaughter was not an annoyance last night when she got home."

"None whatsoever, ma'am. I did not even realize she was home."

"Don't fib to your elders, dear. The Lord will punish you for doing so. Have a good day."

With a fiery blush, Bobbi Jo thanked her landlord for the delicious breakfast, and fled upstairs to brush her teeth and grab her purse. Shortly thereafter, she was on her way to work.

The front door was locked when she arrived at the storage warehouse. Putting her face close to the grimy window, Bobbi Jo peered inside. The lights were on but there was no one around.

She rapped on the glass and waited for the old man to appear.

It took four times, each knock firmer than the one before, to get his attention.

Flipping the lock, he growled, "Stop trying to break my door. Can't ya read? I'm closed today for inventory. Come back tomorrow."

Bobbi Jo's jaw dropped.

"I don't have time to watch you catching flies. So, if there's nothing else, be on your way."

"U-umm, sir, you hired me yesterday to help out."

"I did what?"

"You told me to come and help out."

The old man took a step closer. "Well, if you ain't that girl. I'da never recognized ya dressed like that. Mind, I never expected to see you back in the first place. Woulda thought you'd come to your senses after you left."

He trudged toward the counter, barking, "Don't lollygag about, there's work to be done. By the way, what did you say your name was again?"

"Charlie, sir."

"Don't call me sir. This ain't the military. The name's Butterman. Call me Amos."

"Yes, sir...errr...Amos."

Reaching over the counter, Butterman snatched a painter's cap from a shelf and tossed it to her.

"Put it on, you don't want to mess your hair up."

Bobbi Jo did as he bade, threading her ponytail through the hole at the back.

"Grab a clipboard and that pad of paper by the lift, and head upstairs. The lift is already on."

"What is it you want me to do?"

"List and count the shit up there. What the hell did you think I wanted you to do? Contact the dead, maybe? List the storage number and record what you find in that stall the best you can.

"Oh, and don't open any of the crates or break anything. You do...it comes out of your wage."

"Speaking of which, what *does* the job pay?" Bobbi Jo asked.

"Enough to be taxed on," was Butterman's reply. "Now, get along."

Butterman figured, given the chaos, along with the abundance of spiders who inhabited the warehouse, the girl would run screaming out of the door before the first hour was up.

By midmorning, he was a mite concerned that this had not proved to be the case. He *had*, however, heard the sounds of boots shuffling above him, so he let her be.

At lunchtime, and because it seemed far too quiet, he felt worried enough to venture to the second floor.

He found his new employee at the opposite end of the warehouse. Not announcing his presence, he watched her climb over crates and bulky furniture to examine smaller items at the rear.

Approaching, Butterman saw cobwebs draped from her hat. The fact she did not seem phased by the added decorations made him chuckle, startling her.

"Oh, hey, Amos. Ya scared me half to death."

"I doubt that, girl. How's it going up here?"

"I'm getting there. Not too much left. I can stay late if you need me to."

"We'll talk about that later. Let's take a break and get some lunch. My treat."

Brushing herself off, Bobbi Jo followed Amos to the lift.

Half expecting a bologna sandwich, she was puzzled when he opened the front door to escort her out.

Seeing Bobbi Jo's confusion, Amos said, "Ya don't think I want to eat in that dust bowl do you?" He opened the passenger door of his flatbed truck. "Hop in."

He drove across town to the café where she first met Ginny.

As they entered, that very same waitress skipped over to greet them.

"Hey, Roomie," Ginny chirped then stuck her tongue out at Butterman. "Hi, Amos. You better be treating my girl well."

"Yeah, yeah," he grumbled. "How about you do the same and feed us?"

"As long as you promise to tip this time."

Ginny led them over to a booth near the counter so she could keep an eye on them.

Amos ordered cheese sandwiches and sodas for the both of them.

When Ginny slid the plates on the table, she nudged the old man. "I see you're as generous as ever. Ya could have at least sprung for fries, ya ol' skinflint."

Bobbi Jo came to Amos's defense. "It's okay, Ginny I'm still pretty full from Mrs. McGuire's delicious breakfast."

"Bah." Ginny waved a disdainful hand at Bobbi Jo's lunch companion. "I better see you order this poor girl a slice of pie and ice cream."

Spinning on her toes, Ginny disappeared into the kitchen.

Amos grinned at Bobbi Jo. "Looks like you're getting pie à la mode whether you want it or not."

The two ate in silence for a few minutes, then Bobbi Jo broached the question which had been uppermost in her mind since she clapped eyes on the building.

"Amos, what's with the name painted on the side of the warehouse?"

"Hmm?" Amos raised a brow.

"The name. Buchanan Mercantile. What's the story behind it?"

Amos shrugged, "There's not much to tell. The place used to be a way station of sorts where people stopped to restock supplies before heading over the pass.

"Was run by a mean old cuss, name of Zachariah Buchanan. From what they say, he was as evil as he was crooked. He overcharged for goods and sundries. Hell, I heard he deliberately shorted the Donner party on food, then convinced George Donner himself that his wagon train could make it over the Sierras before the heavier snow started to fall. Well, we all know how *that* ended.

"Anyway, Buchanan ran the place until about 1859,

when a group of silver prospectors took issue with what he was trying to charge for animal fodder. Accusing him of theft, they hung him in the stable that used to sit behind this building. No one in the area bothered to investigate.

"The old bastard's son, Micah tried his hand at running the place, but he wasn't his dad. When the town was finally incorporated in the late 1860s, it brought legit merchants and grocers to the area. There was no way he could compete.

"During the winter of '69, his wife found him hanging from the same rafter as Zachariah. That spring, she changed her name, packed up her house and young'uns, and never returned.

"Various businesses tried to make a go of the place throughout the decades, but nothing really stuck. When I got it, it had been abandoned for about twenty years. It was a steal and given what I use it for, didn't need much fixin' up."

"But why leave the name if it was such a blight on the community?"

Amos paused to drain his soda, in time to see their unordered dessert being served by Ginny who winked at Bobbi Jo and placed the check next to Amos's plate.

"It was just left there as a reminder to merchants that screwing over the customers will eventually catch up to them and cost them everything."

Glancing at his pocket watch, Amos said, "Enough with story time. You need to finish your pie so we can get back to work. Can't trust the mice to count the junk in there properly."

Bobbi Jo gulped a mouthful of ice cream. "*Mice?*"

The pair returned to the warehouse and continued the task at hand. With the extra help, Amos was able to complete the inventory around eight instead of well past midnight...or never.

Walking over to his desk behind the counter, he dug a tattered ledger from the center drawer. Settling into his chair, he stifled a yawn with the back of his dirty hand.

"Damn, I guess that damned Ginny is right, I *am* getting old," Amos griped aloud.

Bobbi Jo propped her elbows on the countertop. Sympathetically, she asked, "What's the matter?"

"Ugh, I don't think I have enough energy left in these old bones to reconcile this crap tonight. I guess we'll have to stay closed another day so I can finish this mess tomorrow."

Bobbi Jo fell silent for a moment considering the likelihood of Amos agreeing to what she was about to propose.

Seizing the bull by the horns, she suggested, "If you show me the method you like to use, I'd be happy to hang around and finish. That way all you have to do is double check the figures when you come in."

Amos rubbed his hairy chin, contemplating the offer. "I don't rightly know about that, Charlie. I've never let anybody do that before. This ledger contains personal info on the people storing stuff here, which they trust me to keep confidential."

"I know I just started, Amos, but I'd hate to see you over-do yourself...and I'm a fast learner."

Amos vacillated for a few seconds, then relented.

He had Bobbi Jo take his seat. Placing the note pads

next to the ledger, he showed her how to run through the storage bins in numerical order and verify the item counts with what was in the ledger.

Bobbi Jo thought it was unnecessarily repetitive, but it seemed important to the old man.

When Amos was finally satisfied that the girl had grasped the concept of his filing system, he pulled her chair, with Bobbi Jo clutching its arms, away from the desk. Without warning, he let go of it in playful celebration, sending Bobbi Jo swirling backwards.

Bobbi Jo squeaked as she saw the room spin around her. Jutting out her feet, she planted them on the floor to stop the wild ride. "Amos, you want me to throw up?" She feigned affront.

Chuckling, Amos rifled through his desk and produced a second key to the main door.

"Make sure you lock up when you're done." Adding ominously, "I better not walk into an empty building tomorrow...understand?"

"Yes, sir, Mr. Butterman." Bobbi Jo threw him a salute.

Before he left, Amos checked the small safe under the counter to make sure it was secured.

"Excuse me, Amos, did you really think I was gonna rob you?" Bobbi Jo tsked indignantly.

"Let's just say, while I don't imagine you'll walk out with heavy, bulky furniture, I don't know you well enough to trust you'll leave my hard earned cash alone."

His cynicism, while...in all honesty...reasonable and expected, kind of hurt her heart.

"And, Charlie," Amos softened his tone. "If you need anything, my number is on the blotter."

Bobbi Jo smiled. "Get some sleep, Amos. Ginny might

die of shock if I tell her you actually have a smidge of benevolence in you."

He pushed open the door, grousing, "That annoying busybody."

Bobbi Jo made quick time running through the count sheets and comparing them with the ledger.

She was amused to discover some of the more outrageous discrepancies. One stall appeared to have grown an upright piano, while another included four large crates which had, apparently, materialized from nowhere.

She left a list of items she wanted Amos to check the next morning.

What Bobbi Jo did then was something she knew Amos would fire her for on the spot.

Starting from March 1, 1964, she began reviewing all the new rentals, amazed at the amount of business Amos handled in a month.

She came across ten entries, obscurely recorded as *Arrived by Carrier*. Of those, seven were marked, *Closed Out*.

The three remaining were on the lower level. Bobbi Jo assumed this was not because they were favored customers. More likely, Amos had been the one left to unload the trucks and did not want to bother lugging the contents up to the second floor.

Studying the inventory for each one, Bobbi Jo found what she had been hoping for. On the thirtieth of April, a truck delivered a consignment labeled *Buckman*.

Buckman...*why did that name sound so familiar?* It

taunted her, but she couldn't pin it down...*Buckman, Buckman.*

Without warning, a memory she didn't even realize she had retained, reared up. She had heard the name on the radio before all hell broke loose on that terrible morning... the announcer's voice echoed in her head...

"...notorious bank robber, Eddy Buckman, AKA Edward Buchanan, led the others to freedom."

Bobbi Jo's mind was engulfed by a barrage of fractured scenes, which threatened to consume her in a swirling vortex of horror.

Fighting nausea, and sucking in lungsful of air, she banished the harrowing scenes to the periphery of her consciousness, but it took several minutes until she was able to regain her composure.

Now was not the time to falter. Now, she needed to focus. Time enough to fall apart later, once the job was done.

Resolutely, Bobbi Jo coerced her brain back to the matter at hand.

According to Amos's notes, he had allocated the shipment to a 5x8 stall in the far corner of the warehouse, documenting three large trunks and a bedroom suite.

The ledger showed the stall had been paid for until the end of December.

Bobbi Jo was disappointed to note there was no contact information pertaining to Mr Buckman, neither was there a forwarding address.

She *did* revel in the knowledge, she would likely be here when he returned to claim his belongings or make another payment.

Whichever he chose to do, she could wait him out. There was nothing left in her life except to wreak justice on Edward Buchanan.

Placing the ledger in the desk drawer, along with the notepads, she scribbled a quick message asking Amos to check her work, adding a promise that she would bring coffee and pastries.

Making a last round, Bobbi Jo locked up, and drove home to the boarding house.

Chapter Eighteen

As the weeks passed, Bobbi Jo proved herself trustworthy and indispensable to Amos. She had gone through the warehouse like a tornado and cleaned the place from top to bottom.

She removed the abundance of cobwebs from the rafters, ushering the colonies of indignant, and unceremoniously homeless, spiders from the building with gentle haste.

When the job was complete, Bobbi Jo was relieved to note the facility had never been a hotel for mice. She thanked Amos for keeping the place rodent free and then punched him in the arm for trying to freak her out.

Before long, Amos had granted her full access to the records, putting her in charge of opening and closing accounts, something Bobbi Jo found to be beneficial in keeping track of Buckman.

Initially, she checked the stall on a daily basis to make sure the contents were still there, but quickly perceived it to be a fruitless endeavor because the man could turn up on her day off.

Having carte blanche with the ledger meant it would be easier to find Buckman, whenever he showed his face.

She convinced Amos that, when an account was closed, the renter had to provide a contact address in case stray items were discovered after they were cleared out.

To mark her as a full member of the staff — following a bizarre ceremony reminiscent of an archaic Masonic initiation, where she had to swear fealty to the warehouse — Amos gave her an apron, name-tag, and the sacred combination to the safe

This also entitled her to monitor payments for the units, be they cash, or checks bearing the customers' names.

As fall transitioned into winter, Bobbi Jo registered she was no longer regarded as an outsider. The locals had begun treating her as though she had lived there all her life.

She became a member of the women's pool club; pressed into service by the team's president, who had refused to take no for an answer after watching Bobbi Jo run the table against a couple of guys who thought they could hustle her blind.

Ginny and Bobbi Jo were inseparable, the housemates — much to Mrs. McGuire's chagrin — bar-hopped the local taverns at weekends, falling into the house at all hours, bumbling about like baby elephants.

Hearing them stumble in above her, the old lady ordered them to quiet down, never failing to add, "It was bad enough when it was just one of you. Now I'm living with **two** juvenile delinquents. Straighten up before I kick you both out."

The girls giggled foolishly, countering, "Shhh....you'll wake the landlady."

One night, while hanging out at the bowling alley, Ginny decided they should join a league, even though neither knew how to bowl, reasoning, "It'll be a great excuse to wear ugly shirts. How hard could it be? All you have to do is drink beer and throw a ball."

That observation doomed their team to the cellar all season, but no one cared because the players just wanted to party with them.

Ginny introduced Bobbi Jo to some of the guys with the sole purpose of hooking her up. For her part, Bobbi Jo enjoyed dancing and double dating with Ginny, but never allowed things to go any further.

By the first snow in mid-December, Bobbi Jo had almost forgotten Edward Buchanan. She had not heard the voices of her mom or Jimmy for weeks, and was savoring a *normal* life.

That all skidded to an abrupt halt one afternoon while she was sweeping around the counter area.

Hearing the newly installed bell above the door announce the entrance of a customer, Bobbi Jo stopped to set down the broom. The voice she heard behind her made her blood freeze.

"Hey, doll, is the old man around?"

She turned, and came face to face...what was left of it... with Edward Buchanan. As the old woman in Oklahoma

City had said, he sported a patch over his left eye like a cantankerous character from an Ed Wood monster movie. Her mouth dropped open.

Not appreciating her expression, Buchanan arched an impatient brow. "What's your problem? You dumb or something?"

The crude insult triggered a series of pictures to flash through Bobbi Jo's mind, like a broken film reel. Everything she had lost, everything she had suffered because of this man ricocheted around her head. Any indecision she might have had regarding Buchanan's fate was obliterated with that one barb.

She schooled her features, and strove to sound unperturbed, "N-No, s-sir. I didn't reckon on anybody showing up this late in the day...especially with more snow on the way."

Buchanan apologized gruffly, "I'm sorry about that, but the dang weather's why I was forced to stop in this one-horse dump. Didn't want to because I need to get my truck over the pass and down to Sacramento before it's snowbound, but with my rental fee coming due, and only God knowing when spring will hit next year, I had no choice."

"I understand, sir. Unfortunately, Mr. Butterman has already left for the evening and I was just about to close up."

Unnerved by his unexpected appearance, Bobbi Jo wanted time to process the tumult of thoughts scurrying around her head. Intent on shooing him out, she saw him rub a hand across his forehead, his frustration clear.

An idea began to percolate.

Deliberately heaving a resigned sigh, she looked at Buchanan as though about to grant him the biggest favor in the world. "Just this once, and since you caught me before

I'd locked up, I'll make an exception to Amos's rule. If you can give me your name, I'll take care of your payment."

Buchanan gave the girl a twisted smile in appreciation. "The name is Buckman...Art Buckman."

A thought struck him and, leaning his elbow on the counter, he narrowed his gaze. "Since when did the old man trust anybody else with his money? You sleeping with him, or something?"

"Hey, I should say not. He's old enough to be my Grandpa," Bobbi Jo retaliated heatedly. "He has just come to—"

Buchanan put his palm up to cut her off. "I really don't care about your qualifications, kid. That's between you and Amos."

He scattered fifty dollars across the counter. "Count it if you need to, but that should cover me until April. Now, if you would be so kind as to point out where Amos stored my trunks, I've gotta get some things out of one of them."

Bobbi Jo pointed at the aisle to the right. "Head down that way and around to the far corner."

"Thanks, doll." Buchanan dug into his pocket. Retrieving a ratty dollar, he dropped it next to the other bills. "For your help."

Nonchalantly, he strode in the direction she had given, breaking into a jaunty whistle.

Remembering what her mom used to say about whistling in a building, Bobbi Jo mumbled under her breath, "You don't have to bother summoning demons, you bastard, there's already one here waiting to send you to Hell."

When the sound of Buchanan digging through his stuff quieted down, Bobbi Jo picked up her leather work gloves and winter coat, and called, "I'm just popping outside to clear the path before you leave. Don't want you slipping on the steps."

This was followed by the clang of the bell as the door opened and shut.

Buchanan could not believe his luck. *Jesus, Amos, you'd have been better off hiring a chimp to run the place. I might check out my neighbors' stuff as well,* he gloated inwardly.

Perhaps later, he had other things to do first. Unlatching the largest chest, he lifted off the top tray and set it to one side. This was followed by four neatly folded woolen blankets.

A crooked grin spread over his face at the piles of Morgan Bank bearer bonds, neatly stacked. He had lost track of how many he and his gang had stolen in the robbery the weekend before they were arrested, or how many he had already redeemed, but was eternally thankful he'd thought to conceal them in this trunk.

Regardless, it was immaterial because there was sufficient to keep him fat and happy for five lifetimes.

Scooping out a handful, he thumbed through them to check he had enough to last the winter. "Come spring, I'll collect the rest and head to Europe."

Fixated by greed, Buchanan failed to discern the stealthy approach of stocking feet. It was not until he heard a grunt, that he turned to see a snow shovel about to strike his head.

Stars exploded before his eyes when it connected, and he tumbled to the ground, bonds flying out of his grasp to flutter across the floor.

"W-What the f-fuck?" he stammered. Squinting to focus, Buchanan saw the girl standing over him, the spade in her hands, preparing to repeat her action.

As she unleashed the swing, Buchanan managed to

block the metal scoop with his left arm, but the blow shattered his ulna. Undeterred by the excruciating pain, he bent one knee and kicked Bobbi Jo in the stomach.

She staggered backward as Buchanan scrambled to his feet, bawling, "I don't know what your problem is, doll, but you're gonna pay for this."

Before Bobbi Jo could dodge, Buchanan caught her in the jaw with a brutal right hook. She rammed the shovel into the floor; the blade screeched across the concrete and stopped her from toppling over.

Unlike the punch Roy had inflicted, she tasted the coppery tang of blood and felt something floating around in her mouth. She spat, and a chunk of broken molar landed on the floor.

Without giving Buchanan time to react, she hoisted the makeshift weapon and, with every ounce of strength she possessed, delivered a crushing blow to the same side of his head. This time, the man dropped to the floor, blood oozing from his ear and his good eye.

Bobbi Jo thought she had killed him.

Until she saw the blood bubbling from his mouth and heard his unconscious groan.

Uncertain how long she had before he woke up...if he ever did...Bobbi Jo knelt down and frisked him, finding a set of keys and a pistol — both of which she appropriated.

Standing, she spotted sheets of paper scattered about, some soaked in blood, and realized she had to clean them up, but that could wait until Buchanan was bound.

Hefting the shovel over her shoulder with a victorious flourish, Bobbi Jo backtracked to the front desk. Shoving a couple of rags in her pocket, she snatched a knife and a length of hemp rope from the storage bin beneath the counter with which to hogtie the killer.

Once satisfied Buchanan was incapacitated, Bobbi Jo gathered the bearer bonds and, although not exactly sure what they were, presumed — if they were worth Buchanan coming out of hiding — they must be valuable. She stashed them in the bottom of the trunk, covering them with the blankets and the tray.

Then she scrubbed the floor and spade clean. "No sense giving Amos any cause for concern...or reason to bitch," Bobbi Jo chuckled, admiring her efforts.

Confident all traces of Buchanan's blood had been removed, Bobbi Jo wheeled one of the carts to the stall.

The chest was heavier than she expected but, employing brute force and no small amount of dogged determination, she managed to maneuver it onto the cart.

Muscles aching and sweat trickling down her face, Bobbi Jo repeated the procedure with Buchanan.

Pushing the cart to the loading dock, she left its peculiar cargo there, and sprinted to the front of the warehouse.

In the customers' parking lot, Bobbi Jo located Buchanan's truck waiting under a thin blanket of new snow.

To her, admittedly uneducated, eyes, it resembled one of the ambulances used during the Korean War, its manufacturer's emblem long since faded, and clearly a vehicle purchased from an army surplus store.

Bobbi Jo opened the rear doors, then jumped into the driver's seat, shivering when a blast of frigid wind whistled through the interior, bringing with it flakes of the budding blizzard.

She fumbled with the keys, her fingers stiff from the bitter cold but, eventually, she managed to slot them into the ignition.

The engine whined as Bobbi Jo pressed the starter button on the truck floor with her foot, but it refused to start. After what felt like an eternity, the old truck fired up. Shifting it into gear, she drove around the warehouse, reversing carefully until she had aligned the back of the truck with the loading dock.

Leaving the engine running, she went to get her own car, parking the Hudson alongside the truck and popping the trunk.

Grabbing Buchanan by the ropes he was trussed up in, she wrestled him off the cart and into the ambulance. He landed with a thud, the shock of the icy air rousing him into a groggy consciousness.

While he tried to figure out why it was so dark and why he was freezing his ass off, Bobbi Jo wrangled the chest into her trunk. Shutting the lid, she returned her Hudson to the front of the building.

Hurrying inside, she scribbled Amos a quick note, in case he beat her to work.

Amos,
I apologize for not making it to the bank in time. A
Mr. Buckman stopped before closing. He paid
through April, and demanded I help him load one of
his crates into his truck.
I have to say his personality matched his face
(knowing Amos would find that funny).
The receipts and payments are locked away.
Cinnamon buns are on you!

See you in the morning,
Charlie

Bobbi Jo planned to bring a thermos of Mrs. McGuire's coffee. Ginny had forbidden her to buy coffee from the café, unwilling to have her best friend poisoned by the swill Bud brewed.

Turning off the interior lights, she locked the front door, and exited through the loading bay ensuring it too was secure.

Bobbi Jo climbed into the truck, put it in gear, drove out of the parking lot, and turned left toward Donner Lake.

The truck trundled along Donner Pass Road to the discordant chorus of Buchanan's outrage interspersed with a veritable torrent of profanities.

"You crazy bitch, what the fuck are you doing?"

"Aww, I'm hurt you don't remember me," she cooed.

"I have no goddamned idea who the hell you are."

"How many five-year-olds have you tried to murder?"

Buchanan fell silent, recollection rearing up in his mind.

"I take it that jogged your memory," she scoffed. "Lucky me."

"No. *No*. **No**. Impossible. Clarence and Daryl told me you froze to death."

"I guess they really were as stupid as you suspected. I can't believe they never bothered to track you down. Didn't they think they were owed? But, it's okay, you don't need to worry whether any of them will find out about your secret stash." Bobbi Jo retorted, squinting into the darkness so as not miss the almost hidden exit onto the trail at the far end of the lake, which the road skirted.

"Why? What happened to them?"

"Let's just say, God served righteous justice upon Roy,

and Clarence discovered that smoking was bad for his health. My only disappointment is that somebody beat me to killing Daryl."

"Look, whatever you have in mind...you don't have to do it. W-We can split the bearer bonds and go our separate ways."

A voice exploded in Bobbi Jo's head, "Don't make any deals with this bastard."

"Shut up, Mom."

"Mom?" Buchanan repeated, *shit, he was dealing with a madwoman.*

"You shut up, too," Bobbi Jo snapped at him.

Buchanan thought quickly. It was probably better to reason with her than goad her. He changed his tone and wheedled, "Your mom wouldn't want you to be doing this. She was so kind to Roy, stitched up his finger real good."

"I told you to shut your mouth, you know nothing about my mother," Bobbi Jo snarled.

"I know she wasn't a killer, she died saving you." Buchanan tried to penetrate the girl's distorted psyche, hoping he could tap into the last vestiges of her humanity or, if that failed, push her over the edge...either option giving him a chance to escape.

"Don't let him sweet talk you," her mother's voice implored. "He can't be trusted, he's trying to trick you into releasing him. He deserves to die for what he did."

He deserves to die... the claim resonated with Bobbi Jo. Images from that dreadful day tormented her. He *did* deserve to die. All four had deserved their fate. From the very beginning, she had accepted there was no turning back, no matter what extenuating circumstances she might have unearthed during her quest for vengeance.

Pushing her mother's insistence that Buchanan was

lying, to the back of her head, Bobbi Jo concentrated on the road, aware they were approaching their destination. Spotting the fire trail leading to the lake, she slowed.

Mentally crossing her fingers that the truck would not get bogged, or worse, snow bound, she turned onto it, ignoring Buchanan's litany of curses as the old vehicle jolted along the badly rutted track.

Suddenly, the trees opened out onto a roughly defined parking area, doubtless used by the rangers. Bobbi Jo hit the brake and the truck slithered to an awkward stop in the mud.

Hopping out, she paused to stare up through the dancing flakes at the looming shadow, which was the mountain, certain she could make out her house, a single light flickering in one of the windows. Simultaneously acknowledging, in the dark and blustery storm, it was nothing more than her imagination.

With no time to linger, she went to the rear of the truck, unfastened the spare tire, and pulled the snow chains from the tire mount.

She rolled the massive, and gratifyingly heavy, tire to the top of the short slope — a natural boat ramp — leading to the lake, hoping the ice had yet to harden and the water was as deep as her father had claimed.

Returning to the truck, she was careful not to stand facing the back doors when she risked opening one, narrowly avoiding its wild swing outward when Buchanan tried to ram his weight against it. Had she been in the same predicament, Bobbi Jo would have endeavored to knock over her captor in the same fashion.

It was a futile attempt, the force of which caused him to tumble out of the truck and onto the snowy gravel.

"Nice try, asshole." Bobbi Jo laughed and, snagging the

rope across his chest, lugged him laboriously across the dirt to where she had left the tire.

Struggling to free himself, Buchanan bellowed for help and mercy; his pleas consumed by the howling wind.

Bobbi Jo stopped, took the rags from her pocket, and stuffed them into his mouth, muffling his cries.

He was a big man and moving him was not easy but, eventually, she had him in position. Threading the tire chains through the rope tethering Buchanan, she looped the other end around the tire, fastening the links together, yanking it a couple of times to ensure it was attached firmly.

The smile Bobbi Jo shot Buchanan was devoid of humor. "Anything you want to say? No? You dumb or something?" Parroting Buchanan's earlier slur.

Her mirthless laughter as she balanced the tire on its rim, intensified Buchanan's conviction that she was unhinged.

Powerless to stop her, his eyes widened in terror, his appeals for forgiveness garbled by the rags.

Relenting, she removed the cloth. "What's that? Drop it? Okay, if you insist."

Giving him no chance to respond, she gave the tire a forceful shove.

Man and tire plunged down the bank. Panicked now, Buchanan gave vent to a blood-curdling screech, which bounced around the lake, coming back to Bobbi Jo in unearthly echoes.

Impassively, she watched his demise unfold and, as she stuck her hands into her pockets for warmth, she felt the gun. Withdrawing it, Bobbi Jo hurled it after the source of all her misery. "Catch, maybe it will speed your passing."

The tire smashed through the ice, the weapon following

with hardly a splash. A surge of glacial, dark water greeted Buchanan, and his lungs screamed for oxygen.

As the unyielding mass of metal and rubber dragged him, inexorably, to the murky depths, Buchanan's fingers scrabbled in desperation, hoping that somehow the gun would fall into his grasp.

On this bleak night…Satan was not inclined to be compassionate.

Shivering, Bobbi Jo stood at the top of the slope until there was no possibility of Buchanan miraculously resurfacing.

Involuntarily, her conversation with Carley's mother came back to her, and she touched her cheek, fingers tracing the almost invisible scars.

No longer a reminder of the worst day of her life, now they symbolized resolution. A balance restored.

As she watched the ripples on the lake smooth to black glass, a welcome hush descending, she recalled a fragment of Latin her father had taught her a lifetime ago…

…a single word… *vindicta — when death isn't retribution enough.*

"Thank you, Dad," Bobbi Jo whispered to the wind, then without a backward glance, climbed into the vehicle and pointed it at Truckee.

When she saw the lights of the town shimmering through the dizzying snowflakes, Bobbi Jo cruised to a slightly angled halt at the side of the road, but did not put the vehicle in park. Jumping out, she let it roll down the embankment and into the trees.

If anyone came across the crash, the open door would imply the driver had escaped injury but had abandoned the truck.

Perhaps getting lost in the blizzard.

Lifting the collar of her thick jacket, Bobbi Jo trudged the rest of the way to the warehouse.

The sprawling building was in darkness, the pristine layer of snow indicating Amos had not come to check on her.

Relief warred with irritation, *didn't he care that she was all alone on a wintry night?* She muttered under her breath about the ingratitude, vowing to chew him out for that oversight, but not right now.

Right now, she just wanted to be home and curled up in her warm bed.

Epilogue

As the long winter finally gave way to spring, the mystery of the truck, abandoned in a ditch outside town following the December blizzard, continued to baffle local law enforcement.

No one had claimed it, and the address on the registration proved to be invalid.

Spots of blood were found in the back, but the coroner ruled the amount was insufficient to suggest foul play.

The spring also witnessed a reluctant yet necessary farewell to Amos and the McGuires from one Charlotte Bernhard — no forwarding address.

When Mrs. McGuire went to prepare Charlie's room for the next tenant, she was surprised to find the girl's suitcase and clothes in the closet.

Propped on the dresser, an envelope with her name on it. It contained a substantial amount of cash and a thank you for her hospitality.

Her body hit the floor with a thud loud enough to pry

her husband out of his paper and up to the third story room at a gallop.

Two Months Later

"Charlie, are we done yet? I want to get to the party on the beach before all the cute surfer guys are taken."

"Did you call your grandmother, Ginny?"

"Not today, but I'll call her before we leave for the Riviera."

Bobbi Jo pinned her traveling companion with an uncompromising look. "*And* once we get there. You know how she worries."

"I promise. Geez, Mom."

"Watch it," Bobbi Jo chuckled and nudged Ginny's shoulder. "Okay, come on, time to have some fun."

On consecutive days, two envelopes — sent from Rio de Janeiro, Brazil — were delivered. One to a boarding house in St Louis, the other to a café on the outskirts of Oklahoma City.

Enclosed, a cashier's check made out to the respective recipient for ten thousand dollars. Clipped to each check, a note proclaiming, *Debt paid in full with interest and eternal thanks.*

Included was a photograph of a woman wearing a

skimpy red bikini, oversized sunglasses and a large floppy hat. She was standing on a beach, ocean waves crashing to the shore behind her.

On the reverse was written, *Having a wonderful time. Wish you were here.*

The astounded beneficiaries, despite being clueless as to the photographer's identity, were delighted and forever grateful that whoever it was had elicited from their friend a genuine smile...

...finally!

About the Author

Rori Bleu

With a smattering of riverboat pirates and royalty in her heritage, Rori Bleu's childhood reflected her past.
An interest in fairy tales, myth and legend were as important as spirited discussions around politics and current affairs — although some might argue they are one and the same!

A fascination, sparked by listening to Grimm's Fairy Tales at her grandmother's knee, not only encouraged Rori's passion for reading, but also steered her into the world of RPG's.
What began as a fun pastime, soon evolved into the creation of fantastical worlds, but Rori never lost her love of politics going on to specialise in Governmental History and Historical Research.

Naturally this means her stories are steeped in historical accuracy and real-life intrigue. While Rori's love of a happily ever after means her preferred genre is romance, don't be surprised if you discover an occasional detour into historical fiction, thrillers, horror and fantasy.

To find more of Rori's books... click the link
https://linktr.ee/roribleu

About the Author
Rosie Chapel

Rosie Chapel lives in Perth, Australia with her hubby and three furkids. When not writing, she loves catching up with friends, burying herself in a book (or three), discovering the wonders of Western Australia, or — and the best — a quiet evening at home with her husband, enjoying a glass of wine and a movie.

Website: www.rosiechapel.com

Also by Rori Bleu

Pineapple Meringue

Imprisoned Hearts

Port of London

Dani's Masquerade

Black Tulips

Ajei's Destiny

Porta Aeternum

The Queen's Heart

Syn *with Matthew Forester*

Echoes and Illusions *with Rosie Chapel*

Evie's War *with Rosie Chapel*

Also by Rosie Chapel

A Hidden Rose — Book Five

The Daffodil Garden

The Unconventional Duchess

Rescuing Her Knight

Elusive Hearts - *An Unexpected Romance*: Book One

His Fiery Hoyden

A Regency Duet

A Regency Christmas Double

Fate is Curious

A Christmas Prayer *with Ashlee Shades*

The Lady's Wager

Winning Emma

A Love Impossible

Unravelling Roana

Love Kindled

Fairy Tale Romance

Chasing Bluebells

Contemporary Romances

Of Ruins and Romance

All At Once It's You

Cobweb Dreams

Just One Step

His Heart's Second Sigh

Dystopian Romance

Echoes & Illusions *with Rori Bleu*